A FROZEN HEART

A BLOOD WAR NOVEL | BOOK 1

ALIA JOHNSON

©A Frozen Heart (A Blood War Novel Book 1) by Alia Johnson

Edited by Aquila Editing
Cover by Christopher Coyle
Artwork by Allen Geneta
Formatted by Lyn Forester

All rights reserved.
This book is protected under Copyright laws. Any unauthorized reprint or use of this material is prohibited. No part of this publication may be reproduced, distributed, or transmitted in any form or by any means, including photocopying, recording or other electronic or mechanical methods without the prior written permission of the author, except in the case of brief quotations embodied in critical reviews and certain other non-commercial uses permitted by copyright laws. For permission requests, please contact the author.
This is a work of fiction. All of the characters, organizations, and events portrayed in this story are either products of the author's imagination or are used fictitiously, and any resemblance to actual events, business establishments, locales, or persons, living or dead, is entirely coincidental.

ACKNOWLEDGMENTS

A big thank you to my family. Thanks for believing in me and letting me type away every day lost in my own world.
Thank you to my betas for sticking with me and giving me great feedback.
All the authors I contacted for advice, thank you for your kind words.

PROLOGUE

Dark clouds boiled over the borders of Merdi and Romule. The sky churned with menace and lightning flashed over the armies that met on the battlefield. It shed tears over blood that had already been lost. This was supposed to be a peaceful meeting to end the feud between two kingdoms. The rulers of both sides met to sign the Blood Treaty. Queen Bera and King Desmond of Merdi sat on their horses on one side. They waited for a surprise attack from their enemy.

King Rion of Romule was across from them. He stared back, worried, since he had everything to lose signing this treaty, while the other side gained all. But the fear for his children overrode all the concern he felt. He feared for the very land they stood on. He couldn't stop what was coming; it was already out of his control. The guilt ate away at him. It made him reach out to Merdi's kingdom, but even he couldn't have expected the events that were about to unfold.

CHAPTER 1

The carriage pulled up to Antiqua. The castle was surrounded by a high wall protecting it from the elements, but the ice still found a way through. The old stone walls had an impenetrable coat of it. Icicles hung across every balcony and outcropping. The marketplace was empty in the middle of the day. Strange, since Odesha remembered a market full of people selling their wares when she was younger. The young guard stationed near the front of the carriage walked around to open the door. He held his hand out to help her down from the high steps.

Odesha nodded and whispered a small, "Thank you."

The guard bowed his head in respect. The guards never spoke to her. She wasn't sure if it was because they had been ordered not to or because they felt pity for her. Either way, she didn't mind the silence. Not anymore.

The doors of the castle crunched loudly as they opened. It was obvious they hadn't been used for a long time. Several servants had to break away the ice blocking the door's path with their shovels. Eyeing the entrance with a cold look, Odesha walked up the steps slowly trying not to slip. She had never seen the ice so thick on the steps. When the doors had first opened, a horrid odor had reached the group standing by the carriage. One guard even coughed in distress at the smell. The castle had not been taken care of. Odesha wasn't sure who was at fault for the conditions of the castle, the staff or Vladeric, but she was going to find out.

More servants waited for the princess inside with their heads bowed. Vladeric, the current overseer of Antiqua, was surprisingly absent from greeting them. Odesha shrugged. She wouldn't want to greet the person that came into her home to conquer either. To the surprise of many, Vladeric was not royalty from Merdi, only a guardsman. He had been promoted above his rank when he had been assigned to Antiqua by Odesha's mother, Queen Bera. To the guardsman he would go back to once Odesha found out where he was hiding in this filth.

A short, brown-haired servant walked forward, curtsying deeply. Her hands shook when she clasped them in front of her. Odesha raised a brow but thought the servant's nervousness was from meeting royalty.

"Welcome, Princess…Princess Odesha. My name is Miravena. A room has been prepared for you if you will…er…follow me, please." Miravena's voice shook with terror, her eyes remaining downcast.

This wasn't nervousness from meeting royalty. No, this was true fear. Odesha could sense it in the air, like a sickness spreading. The guards were concerned, their eyes tracking to every hidden nook to check for danger. They kept their hands on their swords, prepared to fight, if necessary. The servants acted like they were under attack. One servant even flinched away when the carriage driver approached him to inquire where the stables were. Odesha had the sudden urge to find out the reason for the servant's behavior. A stirring of purpose fluttered through her, calling her to solve the mystery of the castle.

Holding tightly to that feeling, Odesha rubbed her chest, feeling the ice buried deep in her heart, not moving. The sense of purpose was new to her, foreign. It was better than feeling nothing. She followed the servant down the hallway, but kept vigilant in case someone hid in the shadows.

The room Miravena took her to was richly decorated. It had recently been aired out, the smell fresher, the window still open. Odesha dismissed the servant with a wave to explore her room, but before she could, exhaustion overcame her. They had been traveling fast across a long distance to reach Antiqua. She slipped off her shoes and fell on the bed. The sleep Odesha fought so hard came with the nightmares she tried to forget. The frozen statues from the ice garden watched her with unseeing eyes in her dreams.

The next afternoon, Odesha stood looking out her window while holding a chalice of blood. As thoughts of the servants and the castle swirled in her mind, she dipped a finger into the red liquid and dragged it slowly across the stone wall. Taking a light sip, she remembered the day she had been sent to Antiqua.

King Desmond sat on his throne, his great girth taking up the entire seat, waiting for his daughters' arrival. He was a patient man, or so he had been told, but at the moment he didn't feel like it. His black horns curled back from the top of his head, hidden in his untamed hair. Dark eyes watched two of his three daughters walkdown the hall. Vashti was tense, her yellow-golden hair bundled tight in a bun on top of her head. She watched him with anger boiling in her eyes from his summons. His decision would help Vashti control her emotions better, he hoped. His first-born daughter, Odesha, was tall and thin compared to her sister. Her eyes were hollow with sadness, even her skin looked dull and lifeless.

After this meeting, he would wallow in his misery in private, but before them he would be strong. He had to be. Sitting up straighter, he strengthened his resolve to follow through with his decisions. To not show weakness and be calm. King Desmond was never weak, but he had to clear his throat several times before his announcement.

His great voice boomed in the large throne room when he took control over himself. "It's time you found your place in the world, Odesha. I know you have been feeling… unwell. I'm giving you Antiqua, the homeland of your mother. I need you to bring the salt mines back." Glancing at Odesha fleetingly, he continued. "Profits have been failing these past years and no reports are coming in from Vladeric." He swallowed roughly, watching Odesha's reaction from the corner of his eye.

She continued to stare up at him with no expression, making his insides shrivel. He was losing his oldest daughter, could feel her time ticking down. There was no emotion in her face.

No spark inside her like he hoped there would be at his announcement.

Odesha had no reason to hold out from the ice encasing her heart. Her mother was gone, and he knew she had told Vashti she had no purpose in Merdi.

This was the only idea he could think of to save her. After trying everything in Merdi to end her curse, he had decided to employ the greatest minds to look at every option for her. But there was nothing that could help his oldest daughter.

The history books were translated. They all said the same: the ice was a gift from Freyja. It was given to a select few who were chosen to enter the ice garden of the Gods. The sprawling garden behind Merdi kept his cursed people safe, their bodies frozen for eternity for their families to visit. They were gone, never to move again, like stone statues. To melt the ice around their heart, a spark of fire was needed. But nothing and no one had sparked the fire inside Odesha, to his dismay.

Until news of distress arrived from Antiqua. When the messenger came, Desmond saw interest light in her eyes. A spark of life. The mystery called to her. He couldn't explain it, but felt deep in his bones this was what he needed to do. He had to send her home to the very ice he was trying to save her from.

Odesha eventually nodded her head to his edict. Her dull eyes turned to her sister. Vashti squeezed her hand tightly to give Odesha the support she needed. They were never separated, it was unthinkable.

Vashti would travel with Odesha, she decided, as plans for their trip together raced in her mind.

Until their father turned to say, "And Vashti, I have another task for you…"

Desmond tore the two sisters apart from each other that day.

Odesha glanced behind her and grimaced at her reflection in the ice. Her snow-white hair flowed down to her small waist, tendrils of hair falling loosely from her braid.

Mother would be disappointed if she could see her now. A small amount of blood trailed from her lips. She swiped it with a finger, a flutter of emotion racing through her at the thought of Queen Bera, but it vanished as soon as it came.

Never perfect. Never again.

A sharp knock at the open door pulled her attention away from the pale reflection.

"My lady, everything has been prepared as you ordered." The voice trembled with the fear Miravena valiantly tried to hide. She waited, in the doorway, for orders from her new lady. So bewitched by the princess's hauntingly sad face, she couldn't pull her gaze even if she tried. Her own plain brown hair and homespun cloth looked dull in comparison. She wore a heavy cloak to combat the cold halls of the castle, but the princess seemed not to be bothered with the chill. Odesha turned to Miravena with sad eyes, heavily framed with lashes. She whispered, "Let us begin."

This was the first Reawakening Odesha had ever led.

Queen Bera, her mother, had been thorough in her teachings, one thing she could be thankful for. There were so many children here. Gliding into the room that Miravena indicated, Odesha marveled at the ice sculptures littering the room. The room, made from ice formations, curved softly. The walls twisted and turned in an artist's sculpture. The inscriptions danced along the ice curvature. They were carved thousands of years ago, before the Blood War, when another family ruled Antiqua.

In the middle of the room, a large pool filled with dark blood waited. The blood's copper smell radiated throughout the room. Odesha's white ceremonial gown trailed behind, swirling eerily. In the corner of the room sat a small sickly child with yellow curls and green eyes. Her breaths pushed heavily from her body, shaking her small frame. The child's mother and father sat on both sides of her. Each held a hand tightly. Their pale, nervous eyes remained locked on Odesha's gaze as she made her way to them.

There was no feeling in Odesha's eyes, and they could see it. That made them worry even more. Miravena followed behind Odesha with shuffling steps.

The princess ordered, "Ready her," indicating the child with a raised hand.

"Yes, my lady," Miravena replied quickly. She moved quickly to follow the instructions to not anger the princess. Miravena placed the child's small hand in her own and gestured towards the robes hanging in the back of the room. The child shakily stood to kiss her parents, and Miravena tugged her away when she finished. The child stumbled, dragging her feet behind her like an invisible tether was holding her back. Once the small girl was undressed, Miravena fastened a dark robe around her. Miravena pulled her gently towards Odesha, who was waiting waist deep in the pool, staring at her own reflection with a pensive expression. The child's sad eyes remained locked on her feet. Her sickly frame shivered while she waited for further orders.

"Child look at me and tell me your name," the princess ordered softly, her own eyes rising from the pool. Odesha fleetingly knew sadness was what the child was feeling. Long ago, the emptiness inside of her had pushed feelings aside as if they were insignificant. There wasn't much time left.

The child complied and held her gaze. "My name is Evie." Odesha tilted her head. The little girl was brave to hold her gaze. There were many that couldn't.

"Evie…will you come in the pool?"

Evie nodded and placed her tiny hand in Odesha's. She shivered harshly.

Odesha's hand was frozen.

Evie glanced back at her parents, becoming more frightened when she noticed small tears trailing down their faces. The lady led the child down the steps, making sure she didn't fall. The thick liquid made it difficult to maneuver. Odesha's legs felt as if they were pushing through thick sludge. The increasing smell around them was making Odesha hungry. Her hands slid under Evie's arms to carry her to the middle of the pool.

"Evie?"

Evie's eyes glanced up to the lady. "Yes, my lady?"

"Repeat after me please." Odesha gently stroked the child's yellow locks, keeping her focused.

"Ye…ye…yes, my lady."

The princess began to recite the ancient rite passed through the ages while keeping her eyes on

Evie. The sacred words were powerful when they echoed through the room. When Evie repeated a phrase, the lady would speak again. Back and forth they continued until the final verse had been repeated back. Odesha motioned for the chalice that Miravena held in her grip. She lowered the child further down into the water, praying to Freyja to help Evie.

"Evie, it's time to close your eyes, little one," Odesha instructed. Evie nodded, looked to her parents fleetingly, and obeyed the ordered words. She emptied the chalice over the child's head and spoke the ending of the Reawakening.

As the last words sounded, Evie's eyes popped open, her small mouth opening to gasp. Odesha pushed her under, submerging her body in the blood. Evie fought back, thrashing. Her screams, silent. Bubbles floated to the surface. Evie's eyes slid closed, her body lax.

She pulled Evie from the pool and watched the blood return to the pool. The droplets sliced through the water.

The cries of Evie's parents become louder.

Miravena rushed to grab the forgotten chalice in Odesha's hand. She hurried back to quiet the parents, hoping they didn't draw the lady's anger, but she was just as afraid as them. Odesha stared blankly at them with furrowed brows, sorting through her own feelings as she tried to understand theirs.

Evie's lips parted in a soft sigh. The breath gently puffed from her small mouth. The change in the child's face was extraordinary. Her green irises now glistened with shards of diamonds, shining bright in the illuminated room. Small silver tears flowed down her face into the pool. The tears made small ripples flow across the blood. Health radiated through a once sickly body.

The blood was now gone from Evie, returned to its resting place in the giant pool. It had left her in the clean robe she had been wearing. Odesha noticed Evie's tears after she turned from the parents. She tilted her head and tried to understand why Evie still cried when the ceremony went so well.

Tears. Tears meant sadness. Odesha remembered them.

"Why are you sad?"

Evie sniffled. "Oh, my lady, the pain is all gone. But…but…did I pass the test?" Choking on a sob, she hid her face in Odesha's robes.

Odesha looked up to Miravena and Evie's parents, who had approached the pool. Confused, she asked, "What does Evie speak of?"

Miravena's face turned a bright red, but she held her gaze bravely. "My lady, Vladeric performed the

Reawakening as you do now, but when the child fought, Vladeric would become enraged. He decided if the child did not accept the transition, they were unfit for life," Miravena added softly. "Several children left to join Freyja, my lady." Small tears leaked from her brown eyes. Her hands trembled with the memories she would never be able to forget.

Odesha tried to understand, her emotions slow and hard to process, making it difficult to form the correct response. "And this is what you thought would happen today?"

They nodded, confusion clear on their faces. "We were so scared, my lady, that she wouldn't pass the Reawakening. She's so young for the symptoms to start."

Taking in their stuttered words, Odesha believed she found the reason for the fear and distrust she had encountered when she had arrived. She knew what she had to do.

Glancing down to Evie, she ordered, "Evie, look at me." A strange feeling was coming over Odesha and she felt uncomfortable. Evie remained still and held Odesha's bright gaze with fresh eyes, clear of fear.

"You will live forever after this Reawakening," Odesha promised.

Evie gasped quietly, lips parting. Her parents

gasped. They had expected to bring home their child's body when she fought the princess in the pool, but instead she would thrive.

Odesha continued, "The Reawakening isn't a test. The pool is sacred, the rites passed down to the children when they change. No person can judge you. That's foolish nonsense from a twisted man, given power that shouldn't have been trusted to him." She shook her head with disgust. "The Reawakening is our way to change a vampire body from consuming human food to drinking blood. A vampire child must live on human food, but once they reach a certain age their body craves blood. The body doesn't know how to handle the change. The Reawakening will stop your sickness by purging your body of human food using the pool. I would never harm a child." Odesha's words ended in a shout. Her emotions emerged through a crack in the ice surrounding her heart. This was what she had been feeling.

Anger. Resentment. Purpose.

When the princess's words sank in, Evie's eyes widened, the fear leaving her. The family's uncontrollable crying had been alarming, but the lady had thought that their sadness was from their daughter's pain. Odesha shuddered, her mind flashing back to her Reawakening and the pain she had felt that day.

"Mother, I fear she won't last much longer," her sister Vashti whispered. She had her arms wrapped around Odesha's thin shoulders to comfort her. Odesha's pale face dripped with sweat, the bed already soaked through from hours earlier. She saw through her tears her mother had her hair in a formal coronation weaving. Her large diamonds swung in the moonlight while she readied to leave them with the guardsman standing nearby. Queen Bera turned to Vashti. She sneered, "Impudent girl, your father and I have been signing the treaty to free the blood slaves in Romule. This is historic for our people. I will get to Odesha when the celebrations are over." Waving her hand in the air, she dismissed them. Mother whipped around in her red gown, leaving Vashti to care for her ailing sister, alone.

Odesha was lucky her father had intervened. She would never let a child suffer as she did that night. Returning to the present situation, the unpleasant memories faded away. Miravena looked at the princess with new hope in her eyes, even though she twisted her hands together.

Straightening her back, Odesha promised, "I am overseer. Vladeric is no longer in control. I am Princess Odesha De Von Desmond of Antiqua and there will be no child's death during a Reawakening.

I am law, and Freyja have mercy on anyone that crosses me." Miravena's fearful eyes reflected what she now saw. Silver eyes glittered with thousands of diamonds, their sparkling intensity blinding during rage. Blood dripped from Odesha's gown, her nails and fangs elongated. She truly resembled the beautiful monster her mother had hoped she would be.

The frozen queen carrying a frozen heart. Alone. Forever.

"Bring me Vladeric," she ordered, flicking her eyes to the guard. It was time to erase the menace from her land.

CHAPTER 2

The guardsman stood at the entrance of the dungeon, waiting for further orders from their princess. Disgust was clearly painted on their faces. The guards that were able to stand the heat of the dungeon were inside securing Vladeric to be questioned. They had never heard of such blasphemy during a Reawakening; it was sickening to their kind. A perverted tyrant had been sent by the hellfire to prey on children, they reasoned. The man had stirred hate and fear among the people of Antiqua. The guards were more than eager for Odesha's judgment.

Odesha paused at the door to the dungeon. Heat pulsed from the metal entrance, even though the door was tightly closed. She instinctively wanted to turn away.

A guard opened his mouth, hesitating to voice his opinion. He hadn't known the princess long, but from what he had seen, she was kind. She didn't show any emotion, preferring to be by herself than in the company of others. That didn't bother him, he had heard the whispers of her curse from others, and only felt sadness for her fate. Her willowy figure was graceful, her gray eyes always emotionless.

Odesha turned to look at the guard when he hesitated, giving him a nod to continue.

"If I may, princess, the heat of the dungeon is... stifling. You can give me your sentence you wish carried out and I'll say them word for word to Captain Philo," he promised, trying to prevent her from the pain she would feel.

Odesha shook her head with denial at his suggestion and paused for the strength to continue. The heat was painful to her, the ice inside her throbbing with retribution if she entered, but she would go through it for the people. Odesha was their voice and it was her job to care for them. The dead and the living. The questioning and the judgment she would carry out herself.

"No. I must go in and speak with him. Thank you for your consideration," she acknowledged absently, staring miserably at the door. Rubbing at her chest, she kept asking herself why didn't she train with heat again. Taking a deep breath, bracing herself for what she was about to face in the room, she nodded to the guard to open the heavy door for her. Both guards moved to the handles and grasped them, straining to open the door. It felt like a fire blazed across her face when the air blasted from inside. She instantly felt the sweat gather on her back. A trail began to drip. A headache began to form, slow and insidious with its throbbing. The ice stabbed her across her chest, like tiny needle pricks attempting to warn her against entering.

Vladeric was chained between two posts, anchored to the ground, unable to move. His pale, sweating face was how she remembered him from the last time she had seen him in the throne room of Merdi. Only a few feathered lines on his forehead showcased his advanced age. His sharply pointed nose was what she remembered, like a hawk waiting for the mouse to show itself before it struck. The hair he usually kept neatly styled was standing on end as if he had put up a fight to be restrained. The sneer he directed towards her was full of contempt.

Odesha walked towards him. The heat made her feel like she was moving slower than she really was. It was hard to do, but she would push through it. She repeated that in her head over and over to convince herself.

"You," Vladeric bit out harshly.

"We haven't met. Trust me. I would remember," she countered. She wouldn't let the coward scare her.

He eyed her body up and down disdainfully. "I remember the sniveling coward of a child Bera hid behind her skirts in court," he remarked, meeting her gaze with his own. "The useless twin. At least your sister had a spine in her." He reared his head back, spitting at her feet, but missed by a couple of inches. Yes, this man had changed, she decided. He had been corrupted by the power given to him, as many others before him had. She ignored him, used to the whispered comments in Merdi, asking instead, "Why would you harm those children? Those aren't our ways."

Even she couldn't imagine him doing something so atrocious to small children.

"I am *royalty* from Romule. Did no one ever tell you that? This isn't my way. Blood and power are revered in my home. I needed the blood. That intoxicating, pure blood. Blood is what powers the magic we wield." He tilted his head as if to smell the air, inhaling with pleasure at the thought of killing. A monster hidden behind a beautiful face. The whole time he had been here, he had been using the people to harvest the blood. Her mother had let him in her own home and set him loose on the people.

Odesha's knees began to weaken, the heat overtaking her. She wasn't going to last much longer and needed to end this confrontation before she fell over. The last image she wanted him to remember would be her back, turning away from him and his ways, confident and strong.

"I sentence you to death for your crimes, Vladeric. You will not have a burial befitting of your station because you now have no station. You will die a pauper. A criminal. Enjoy your return to the hellfire. There will be no blood or magic there." She moved away from his menacing gaze. The answers to her questions had been found and he had admitted his own guilt to the room. Her guards moved to do her bidding. The order hadn't said how she wanted him to die, though. She hoped her guards could be creative with how Vladeric met his end because she didn't have the strength to think of ways he could suffer.

Vladeric's mocking laughter stopped her retreat from the dungeon. "You think you know what is coming for you? For all of you," he shouted. "My family will avenge me once they hear of my death. The Blood Treaty is only a piece of paper and you risk losing even that by your order! What would your mother think?" His smile turned sinister. He added, "Did you know who her secret lover was? I do. He is the one who sent me to Merdi."

There was only one person that could be. If Vladeric was royalty, only King Rion would be able to order him anywhere. She thought of her father and the suffering he had gone through over the years after losing her mother. Desmond blamed himself for Bera's death, turning to his brew for solace in the years without her, never knowing the person who had crushed her heart and caused her death. The ramifications were staggering.

Vladeric's smile grew larger, more menacing. His eyes became wild when he added, "It was a shame he married another. What is coming for you was forged long ago. It was made to bring destruction."

"I know what is coming for me. I stopped fearing it years ago. Fear your own fate," Odesha whispered to herself, her back still facing him. She continued through the open doorway, motioning for the guards to close the doors on her final words. Once closed, she leaned her head against the cooler metal, listening to the cries of anguish from Vladeric's mouth. It wasn't close to what the families had suffered, and Endemion, her brother, wasn't here to ensure it was brutal, but she did what she could. What was right. Endemion would support her in that at least if she had just caused the Blood War to begin again.

Vladeric's cries of mercy still bounced in her ears while she walked to check on Evie. Odesha hoped she never forgot those screams. There was a lesson to be learned from this day. To not trust what she couldn't see. Her mother had trusted the wrong people. That trust had resulted in her death. There were evil people everywhere in this world, and Vladeric had proven that they lurked around every corner and every kingdom.

Evie seemed to be in good health, her small body was already recovering from the ceremony. Her baby fangs were starting to sprout early, and her family was in good spirits. They thanked Odesha profusely. Odesha left the family alone to enjoy the castle before they returned to their cottage.

She felt a shiver of anger flow through her, directed towards her mother for sending Vladeric there. Evie would have been destroyed by Vladeric if Odesha hadn't been in Antiqua. This was Bera's ancestral home. Why would she place Vladeric in charge to terrorize her own people?

She had been just a child when Bera had died. In Odesha's mind, her mother was perfect; her spoken word, law. Vashti had tried to argue otherwise. The two sisters had gotten into many fights over Bera.

The memories were making Odesha face some hard truths about the woman she had idolized. Maybe Vashti was right all those years. She had shrugged off Vashti's concerns without reason, hurting Vashti in the process. Odesha would make it up to her the next time she saw her. She would listen.

Odesha walked the halls to her barren room, thinking back to the day Vladeric had been assigned to Antiqua.

"Vladeric. Come forth," Queen Bera intoned. Her appearance was perfect, as always, in the throne room in Merdi. The décor, showcasing the riches Father had acquired, glittered in the dull candlelight.

The court attendees stood silent, divided, standing like statues on the sides of the room, guarding their king and queen. They were all vipers, waiting to strike in the dark when you least expected it, when your back was exposed.

Vashti and Odesha sat behind their parents, trying to stay out of sight in the shadows. They peeked through the slits in the throne chairs, seeing Vladeric, mother's guardsman, march forward. His lithe body moved like a snake, his patrician face preening at the recognition in front of his peers.

Father warned them long ago to stay away from him, reminding his daughters, "His darkness would infect even Freyja's soul."

They took Father's words to heart, too young to know

what he meant at the time. Vladeric didn't look any different from the other guards that protected them.

Queen Bera continued, "I have assigned you to Antiqua, my ancestral home. When I arrive, we will rebuild the salt mines even stronger now that our people are free. The wealth of Merdi will continue to feed our people." The cheers around the room become deafening. It made the girls cover their ears. Odesha looked to their father's face, seeing the anger flash through his eyes for a moment. It disappeared just as quickly. She glanced at Vashti in confusion and shrugged her shoulders, asking a silent question. Why was father angry? Vladeric gave an elegant bow in acknowledgment, gracefully removing himself from the room to follow his queen's orders. He never looked back. Desmond never sent out inquiries on Antiqua's welfare, ensuring their fate. The night Vladeric left for Antiqua was the night Queen Bera fell to her death.

Odesha shook herself out of her nightmare. Vladeric was dead now, there was no reason to reminisce on the past. There was no way to change it.

Odesha's parents were the rulers of Merdi, fighting to end the Blood War together. It was Queen Bera's obsession, forging the treaty and freeing her people. The one good deed, before her death, to Merdi and Antiqua.

The Blood War had started in a dungeon long ago. The magisters of Romule experimented with blood and found out vampires had a unique agent that made black magic more potent. They captured more vampires day after day in secret. The magisters had trouble keeping the prisoners hostage, though. Many of the vampires escaped to warn King Desmond, to report what was happening in the neighboring kingdom, to beg for help.

That's when the heat dungeons were built. The magisters had constructed them to hold vampires and drain them of their blood. They became intoxicated on the magic and the power they wielded. Until the captured vampires began to build a tolerance to the heat and fought back, killing many magisters. King Rion surprised King Desmond when he called for a truce during the war.

Father ordered his children to train with heat in case they were ever imprisoned or exposed to the dungeons. He feared for his children's safety. Vashti was always training, but Odesha never went. She knew the ice was going to be her fate long ago. The heat only caused her pain.

Thinking of her father sent a jolt through her heart. She missed her family every day, not used to being without them. When her father had separated Odesha from the one person that kept her heart from completely freezing, it had been hard for her to cope with the loss even though she never showed it.

Vashti was her lifeline. Basic emotions seemed harder to grasp as time ticked by, but being around Vashti had helped somewhat. Now Odesha had no one. She battled the ice every day, praying to the great goddess Freyja she didn't freeze completely until the task that was given to her was complete.

Father had remarried a beautiful and kind woodland fey after losing Bera. Rube had given birth to her two half siblings and showered her step-children with kindness. Odesha's half brother and sister remained in Merdi but had never been as close to her as Vashti. They had shared a womb together, after all. They were fraternal twins.

Her brother Endemion was dark and mysterious, while Saphira was lost to her own explorations, choosing creatures over people.

Vashti had told Odesha she wasn't surprised that Father had decided to send her here. Antiqua was ripe with salt mines that had turned a heavy profit for the Crown in the past. Since Vladeric had arrived, the profits had dwindled. Merdi's coffers needed the extra profit from the mines to support the people.

Reminded of the mines, Odesha sighed. Now that Vladeric was taken care of, that was next on her agenda. She had to see what Vladeric had done to the mines to stop the profits. That was the main reason she had been sent there. She secretly hoped it was only bad management and a quick fix. Then she could go back to Merdi to be with her family in her final hours.

Opening her doorway, she lit the candles lining the room. After throwing her stiff, bloody gown across the room, she climbed in the large claw foot tub to soak in the cool bath water prepared by the efficient Miravena. She reminded herself to thank the servant in the morning. Looking down at her body, she seemed small in this large tub even though she was tall compared to most people. So pale, her thin body had nary a mark. Her small waist made her small breasts look passable.

A perfect bargaining chip for Father to one day use, she reminded herself. Father was unpredictable, but Brother would never let that happen. Who would want a frozen princess in charge of a frozen wasteland? Her time was limited. When she was back home, she would join Freyja in the ice garden with the other statues.

After bathing, she pushed herself out of the tub and walked over to her wardrobe. She picked out a pale pink gown to sleep in. The candles she blew out left a small puff of smoke. When the smoke stopped, she closed her eyes to sleep, but this time, she willed herself not to dream. The nightmares of the ice garden crowded her mind, making her afraid to sleep. To see them all waiting for her.

A constant peck on the window startled her awake. She was thankful for the interruption. She was dripping with sweat after being chased through her memories, her hand pressed to her breast to slow her breathing.

A large evian sat on the other side of the window. It was a bird used to send messages through the kingdoms. The birds had been used a lot during the Blood War to send messages of all types across territories. Families separated utilized them the most to keep track of one another. She released the latch on the window, letting the evian fly in to land on her mirrored table. He chirped and fluffed his dark feathers, holding out a clawed leg. Lighting a candle stub helped her to see a package attached to the leg.

Odesha didn't have an affinity for animals like Saphira. Her sister could talk to animals all day without stopping to rest. It surprised guests and courtiers alike when they realized she wasn't speaking to them when she passed. Odesha reached for the package slowly to not startle the evian. Eventually the package dropped to the table after several tugs at the knot. The evian hopped away with another chirp. She took a couple pieces of breakfast left by Miravena and placed them beside the bird. It trilled with happiness. Unwrapping the package, she discovered letters from King Desmond and Saphira, but she looked closer inside to see if Vashti had sent her anything. A small silver necklace attached to a note caught her eye.

"If in need, use me – Vashti," the inscription read. Vashti must have stolen some of father's brew to drink again because it was barely legible. The necklace glittered prettily in the candlelight. The end of the necklace held a small crystal, but a shadow caught her eye. A lone speck of blood was in the center. A frozen tear trailed down her face when she figured out the crystal was a bloodstone. She absently swiped the small tear, holding the necklace up to the light to see it better, and whispered, "Thank you, Vashti."

The sacrifice Vashti made of sending the necklace to her caused the ice to warm around her heart. If in the wrong hands, the necklace could be disastrous. Odesha could summon Vashti at any moment. Until the blood dried, Vashti would be by her side. To an assassin, it was priceless.

She read over each letter, wrote replies to all three, and attached them back to the evian carefully to not hurt it. The evian flew out of the window with a harsh push of wings, showing its great strength. The bird disappeared on the wind to return home.

Her heart may just have a little more time if the tear was any indication. She had felt…something… when she saw the lone drop.

Relief? Happiness? Odesha wasn't sure.

CHAPTER 3

They were scheduled to visit the salt mines today. Walking to the waiting carriage, Odesha displayed her royal status, in part thanks to Miravena's help. Her thick winter dress, lined in fur, flowed in the breeze of the cold day. The bloodstone was clasped around her neck for protection. Free of its bonds, her white hair, always glossy and straight, hung down to her waist. A small diamond coronet sat on her head, glinting in the pale light. She wanted to make a good impression on the people her first day out of the castle.

Before dressing, Odesha drank an entire chalice of blood to help her get through the day. The blood helped her gray eyes shine with life. Thirst wouldn't affect her this day.

While they walked to the carriage, Miravena

made small talk with the princess, her previous reticence gone in the new morning. Odesha's personal guard stood beside the carriage. The only guard she knew by name was Captain Philo, since her brother had personally selected them, but she was determined to learn the other names. A new respect had entered their eyes since yesterday. They knew the pain she had suffered, but she had braved the dungeon beside them.

After assisting the women into the carriage, Philo ordered the driver to move out. As they traveled, Odesha admired her new countryside. The mostly flat lands of pure white snow sparkled from the pale light. Dark snow trees twisted and turned high in the air. Large, dangling icicles gleamed, holding on tightly to their branches. In the distance, the salt mines rose from the ground in giant waves, making her wonder what was on the other side. She didn't remember anything listed in the history books she had studied. As far as the books were concerned, Antiqua was the end of Kaia, their world.

Miravena secretly watched the princess staring raptly at the countryside, thinking it was miraculous Antiqua received such a gift. The beautiful lady looked ethereal in the carriage. Her grace and demeanor were intimidating, though. Odesha turned to Miravena, feeling her gaze. She quirked a lip up slightly, trying to appear more approachable and softly complimented the fidgeting young woman, "Thank you for breakfast this morning, Miravena. You are always efficient."

Miravena's nervousness increased, but she tried to appear confident, sitting straighter in her seat. "Welcome, my lady." They lapsed into a comfortable silence, until Miravena cleared her throat to ask, "My lady, could I tell you about Antiqua?" Odesha motioned for her to proceed, giving Miravena her full attention. Odesha's nails remained retracted, her stormy gray eyes calm, helping Miravena gather the courage to continue.

Smiling, trying to mirror Odesha's confidence, she began her story. "I wasn't alive for the Blood War, but I do remember the time when your mother was alive. Before Vladeric came, we lived in small villages around the castle doing day-to-day tasks. When he arrived, his men started to sort us into workers, villagers, and castle workers. He was secretive at what he was doing in the castle; we hardly ever saw him. Then one day, he emerged. Cruel, heartless. He made the people mine day after day. Our healers strained themselves to keep the people healthy. Some said they preferred slavery over his treatment. Some tried to escape to Merdi to send word of the conditions, but Vladeric had them cut down. So, we tried going over the mountains. Many didn't return. One of the miners came back from a search over the mountain. We learned there were monsters on the other side. Giant birds guarded Kaia's borders. The guard described a forest, shrouded with their nests high in the trees. The people that escaped over the mountain…all gone." Miravena turned pink in embarrassment, adding, "I don't mean to talk so much, my lady. I just wanted to give you our history, so you know what to expect when you arrive. These people have been through much."

Odesha reached over the seat to grasp Miravena's hand. The frozen appendage caused Miravena to gasp.

The rumors were true, the princess was frozen.

Odesha ignored Miravena's surprise, replying, "You've been extremely helpful since my arrival by assisting me any way you could. I hope to repair the people's trust, but I need to know the threats. The birds…do they pose a danger now?"

Scrunching her nose, Miravena answered, "I have only heard of sightings of birds farther up the mountain. None have come down to the village as long as I've been alive."

Odesha imagined a giant bird flying down to Antiqua, sitting back hard against the seat with worry.

Another concern. A giant bird attack. Hellfire, what she wouldn't give to have Endemion here to figure out this mess, she thought to herself.

Miravena leaned in conspiratorially, gaining confidence by the minute. "They call the bird 'orik,' after the champion fighter from history. They say the bird has giant plates on its body, like what Orik wore fighting. Gray feathers make it hard to spot when it flies. It has a beak, as a long as a tree. They say the clawed feet are as big as a wagon." She held up a hand, forming claws, growling. Miravena's avid storytelling caused Odesha to crack a smile. She would've laughed out loud at one time in her life after such a demonstration. Now she could barely smile. The ice had changed her so much, she didn't even know who she was anymore. Odesha gazed at one of the snow trees trying to picture an orik, turning her troubled thoughts away from her personal problems.

What other creatures were hiding behind that mountain?

They arrived at the salt mine, stepping out of the carriage, assisted again by Philo and his men.

Miravena indicated where the head miner lived; his home was carved in the side of the mountain. The scarred wooden door was closed tight against intruders. Odesha motioned to the doorway. Before the door opened, she attempted to straighten her appearance to give a good first impression to the head miner. Philo knocked loudly.

The skinniest man Odesha had ever seen opened the door. His tuft of frazzled gray hair stuck straight up in the air like it was waving hello to the group. His too large spectacles sat on the end of his nose peering up at them curiously. Odesha cleared her throat to introduce herself, when the man gasped. He grabbed his chest and fell back on his bottom in the snow. The guards rushed to help him up, but the man waved them away.

The older man pointed a bony finger at Odesha. He shouted out, "Me thought a ghostie was hauntin' me. Me old heart stopped beatin'!" His garbled accent made it hard to understand what he was saying.

Odesha pressed a hand to her chest, confused by what he had said. She reassured him, "Sir, I can assure you I am no ghost. My guard can vouch for me. They've been protecting me for days now."

The guards nodded their heads, agreeing that the princess was not a ghost.

The man harrumphed to himself. He stuck his hands in his overly large pockets, filled over the top with knick-knacks, and remarked, "Supposin, you be the princess. Be thinkin' you were your mum lookin' just like her, standin' there in her fancy frippery."

Odesha winced slightly. She asked, "You knew my mother, sir?" The stories she had heard of Bera's past made her cautious.

He nodded his head decidedly. "Knew her since the day she was borned. Worked in the castle with her parents. Good people, her parents. Sold her to the highest bidder, didn't they? But the gal wanted a big ol' name for herself."

His boldness made Odesha speechless for a moment. Miravena worried her lip with her teeth in distress. She looked back and forth between the two. Even Philo tensed at their stare down.

Suddenly, Odesha's lips formed a small smile in response. She agreed, "Sir, I believe that's the most accurate description I've heard of her yet. If one day you have the chance to meet my father, I believe he would agree."

The old miner's booming laugh echoed through the clearing. The guards stepped forward to grab his small arms. They hefted him to a standing position with harsh grunts, suggesting he weighed more than his slight frame showed. Shaking off the guards supporting him, he linked his arm with Odesha's. He pulled her with him against the protest of her companions. She quickly waved them off, having too much fun with her new friend.

"May I ask your name, kind sir?" She wanted to know everything about the head miner that had known her mother.

He sighed dramatically, "Me mum gifted me with the name Gamble." Looking at her pointedly, he waited for her reaction.

This made her pause in their journey to the salt mine. She stopped walking, sure she had misheard him. "Gamble, sir?" It sounded as if she strangled on the word.

He continued to pull at her arm, his tuft of hair bouncing in distress on his head. She looked at him in disbelief when he yelled loudly to her, "Right! Gamble. Cuz me mum liked to gamble and me mum liked me." His bushy eyebrows wiggled on his forehead, making her smile. Not wanting to hurt his feelings, she smothered an unexpected laugh with her free hand. The guards, however, had no reservations and howled with laughter. The warm feeling across her chest felt wonderful, unknown to her.

"Gal, you'll be wantin' to meet the miners, I reckon. Mira there has been tellin' ya stories, I be thinkin'. And they're probably a mite right, but we've been hearin' some too. The boys are eatin'. Best time to be a-makin' your frippery talk."

"Mr. Gamble, that sounds perfect," Odesha quickly added. "When would be a good time to speak about the low profits from the mines?" She wanted to start working on the problem as soon as possible.

Gamble looked startled, almost falling over again, but Odesha gripped his arm, prepared this time for his nervous stumble so they both didn't fall. "Gal, the profits have been boomin' since the mines been workin'. Now ain't that mighty grand?" He toothily grinned up at her, holding a thumb up. He waited for a response from her, but none came. She stared at him blankly, even when his eyebrows started to wiggle again.

Confusion swamped Odesha. This was the exact opposite of what had been reported in Merdi, but before she could ask, Gamble stumbled away from her, finding his new victim. He ran clear across the clearing, yelling at a poor man hunched over his lunch. He loudly asked if the man was working tomorrow.

What an easy-going man. If the court at Merdi had heard the way he spoke to her it would have been a death sentence. Here she felt…free. The missing profits still worried her, though. She would have to get to the bottom of the mystery. Odesha rubbed her chest, feeling her heart tingle. She observed the new clearing Gamble had taken her to. The large cavernous entrance the miners used was in the distance. The bright torches seemed to go on endlessly. Long tables sat in front of the entrance as families mingled during their break. Some families noticed Gamble as he walked by and sent greetings to him. He returned their greeting just as loudly. He knew everyone by name, that was obvious.

One curly head caught her eye. Evie waved frantically with her family. They smiled at Odesha brightly when she waved back. Evie pointed at her baby fangs and wiggled her eyebrows like Gamble had. Odesha smiled slightly. She felt her chest warm in happiness, causing her to gasp.

Happiness? Was she happy here alone? Could she be? Odesha would have to study these new feelings closer in private, not sure what was happening to her. Were the people her spark?

A nervous energy filtered through the crowd when people noticed her. Some even turned white with fear. The miners tried to shield the small children, fearing she was like Vladeric, even though the new rumors said she wasn't.

Odesha waved to Gamble to let him know she was ready for her "frippery," as he called it. He let loose a loud call used to gain the miners' attention. The people next to him winced. Their hands rubbed their ears, while they shook their heads at him. They were obviously used to the head miner's quirks.

Gamble nodded his head so hard his glasses almost fell from his nose. People gave him their full attention, while he busily straightened his mismatched vest. "All of yous listen to the princess's frippery."

A clap of his hands echoed loudly in the silence. Gamble turned to Odesha to wait for her speech. The people turned an incredulous gaze to her at that statement, trying to understand what Gamble had meant. Odesha subconsciously straightened her appearance, stepping up to where most people could see her. One thing Father had taught her was how to command a room.

Miravena watched her princess approach the tense crowd. Her presence filled the area with her hidden light. The confidence she showed the crowd made Miravena feel proud to call her their ruler. Odesha bared her beautiful teeth in a semblance of a smile to draw the audience in and make them feel more comfortable with what she was about to say.

"My people, yesterday the tyranny of Vladeric was eradicated. His remains are no more! My father, King Desmond, loves this land. With the passing of my mother and close family members, this land fell to the king many years ago." Odesha cleared her throat with a gentle cough. "He recently gifted it to me. My name is Princess Odesha De Von Desmond. I will strive to the best of my ability to be a fair overseer. I hope you will give me a chance to prove myself and settle any misconceptions. The stories I have heard of your suffering have touched me deeply. I promise, as long as I am overseer of Antiqua, I will keep you and your children safe. Thank you." Miravena looked around, trying to get an idea how the people felt about their new princess. It was a short speech, but to the point. She hoped the people heard the princess's underlying meaning. Most of the people were content but whispered behind their hands to neighbors and friends. The princess waved regally to her new subjects. Miravena's heart swelled, because it finally felt like everything was going to get better. Antiqua had a ruler they could be proud of.

Odesha mingled with the miners and their families,

learning their stories. Some were so heartbreaking it made a tear track down her face when they shared their sorrow from the hardship they had faced from Vladeric.

Surprisingly, many couples she met were a mixture of different species. This cohabitation astonished Odesha, after she recalled prejudices her mother had tried to force on her. Lines were drawn between species in court, it had never changed. Odesha met with demons, humans, and even a woodland fey, bundled up tightly to protect herself from the cold. Her frozen heart beat loudly at the love and companionship this close-knit crew shared. She invited many to come to the castle in the coming days, while Miravena jotted their names down in a small book she carried. The lunch bell dinged, signaling the miners' return to work. The guards moved to bring the carriage around at her order. Odesha sent Miravena off on her own task to speak with Gamble to schedule a day he could discuss the mines' profits further, not wanting to keep the miners from their job or from talking with their families; that would be rude.

The families were packing their bags, saying their goodbyes to return home, when Odesha heard the scream. She raced towards the sound and looked up in horror. A massive bird circled the families on the edge of the clearing. The only thing it could be was an orik. It was exactly as described.

Miravena hadn't underestimated their size. Odesha's mouth dropped opened when she saw the sheer length of its body. It was the most menacing creature she had ever seen. The metal plating ran down its face, reaching as far as its toes. The sharp plating gleamed against the snow. The eyes were purely black. It threw its giant head back and let out a piercing screech that made Odesha's ears pop. The face was reminiscent of a stork that called the lakes of Merdi home.

The giant wings flapped towards the ground, sending massive feathers through the crowd, which blocked the path of people trying to escape. The massive orik began a rapid descent from the sky, toward little Evie who was running, arms outstretched, to her parents. The parents were behind Odesha, running as fast as they could to save their child. Time seemed to turn slowly. Odesha measured the speed of the bird and the distance of Evie's parents in her mind.

They wouldn't make it in time.

But she could.

Odesha put out a burst of speed. Her legs pumped hard through the snow. She held arms out to reach Evie. The speed, gifted from her vampire side, pushed her forward, using a large amount of her energy. She enfolded Evie in her arms, holding her tight. Once Odesha turned her back on the bird, the giant wings brought it even closer. The horrid breath ruffled her hair and she knew she was out of time. Throwing Evie to her parents as best she could, she hoped they would catch her. They were almost in arm's reach. The people continued to scream in terror around her, while trying to reach safety. It was so chaotic around them, Odesha couldn't see if Evie had been caught or if she was safe.

The bird's talons closed over Odesha, crushing her in its grip. Her scream of pain echoed across the clearing, while the bird screeched back in triumph.

Miravena watched in terror, held tight by Gamble, who was busy yelling obscenities at the bird. They felt helpless in the face of the giant beast. There was no way they could fight those giant talons. The people scattered, running for cover, trying to save their families. The guards, returning from retrieving the carriage, were blocked by mounds of feathers and the stampeding crowd. They tried pushing through them, shouting orders, trying desperately to reach Odesha. She thrashed in the bird's grip, trying to loosen its hold. Blood began to drop to the snow from the hard struggle. The bird flapped its mighty wings to push off from the ground, holding tight to its captive.

And then they were gone.

Odesha felt disoriented when she woke up. Her head felt like a great anvil was on top of it, forcing her head down. The pressure change from the orik's takeoff was excruciating to get used to. Odesha felt her nails lengthen, her fangs extending, when she reached towards the bird's leg to injure it.

She forgot the feet and legs were all metal plated.

Screams tore from her throat when her nails broke away from the tips of her fingers. The blood flowed from the damaged area. The metal was impenetrable, she realized. She used all her strength to pry apart the long talons holding her, but they snapped back just as quickly. She couldn't budge them. Terrified, she thrashed, until she felt a talon digging into her side. Her movement instantly stopped. She was stuck for the duration of the ride, positive she wouldn't survive being cut in half. The blood loss would be her undoing. She shoved the talon aside, taking a breath of relief when the pain lessened. Dangling, she found some humor in the situation. She could always summon Vashti and they could fly together, but she doubted that was what her sister had in mind when she sent the necklace. It still made Odesha laugh at the thought. A realization made her delighted laughter stutter to a stop. When was the last time she laughed without Vashti? She couldn't remember, but it made her happy all the same.

Even if she was flying to her death.

CHAPTER 4

Odesha kept her eyes open while she dangled. The pain and vertigo became harder to ignore. Her head felt like she had been drinking too much of her father's prized demon brew. If her eyes would hold still, she would be rolling them. In her blurred vision, she saw the salt mines disappear behind her. A large snow tree forest loomed in the dark distance. It looked menacing with its sharp branches reaching out to her.

So many trees, she thought vaguely. She could hide there…

The bird reached the forest and stayed high to avoid the sharper branches. The massive body wove in and out easily. She thought she was dizzy before, but this was even worse. They wove back and forth until the orik decided to slow. Groaning to herself, she lifted her head to peer into the forest to see where she had been taken. She felt like she was about to be sick. The orik suddenly surged upwards, forcing her head down, causing her to clench her teeth. This orik was lucky she was a vampire. If he would have snatched a human, they would have been dead by now. Snorting, she realized she was dizzier than she thought. The bird's priority was not to keep her alive.

The orik abruptly shoved it wings forward, making her body swing helplessly. It began to descend while she watched where she was about to land, hoping to ease her fall.

Odesha held her hair away from her face and saw a circular knot of snow trees bunched together. The black tree branches had been fused together to create large bundles that were bigger than Merdi castle's courtyard. Her hope of getting free increased, until she glanced around and saw more knots spread out on the tops of trees.

Nests. The knots were orik nests. It was going to leave her in its nest, she realized. She was only feet above the nest when the orik opened its talons, threw back its head, and dropped her with a loud screech. She let out her own scream as she fell straight down, landing in an undignified heap in the dirty nest. The filthy gown flew over her head obstructing her view. She shoved it aside and quickly jumped into a squat position to defend herself. The only defenses she had were her broken nails and extended fangs. Her speed could help her run in circles around the nest, but it wouldn't help for long. To her surprise, the orik flapped its mighty wings and flew off through the trees, out of view. She had thought the orik was going to try to eat her then and breathed a sigh of relief that it hadn't. Her eyes darted around in panic at her surroundings, while she tried to reason with herself. She was in a giant bird nest. The survival training she had been forced to attend would have helped, if she hadn't snuck off with Saphira and Vashti to ride horses that day. Giant mounds of feathers lined one side of the nest. Black egg shells covered the entire bottom. The broken shells crunched noisily under her booted feet when she had fallen. There wouldn't be a chance to sneak out of the nest quietly.

And it looked like the baby orik had already hatched. Odesha tried to control her breathing as her panic escalated until she took a step backwards. A sharp pain in her side caused her to hunch over with a groan. The wetness she grasped felt cold. While searching for the source, her hand came away with blood from a wound in her side she hadn't felt yet. Oh, Freyja. The talon had pierced her side deeper than she had originally thought. It must have been the adrenaline that blocked her from noticing. The pain shooting up her side became more noticeable as the adrenaline faded away.

She pulled her gown away to get a better look at the wound. A long, dirty cut in her gown opened to a healing wound that ran down her waist to her thigh. The wound had caused a trail of blood that dripped down among the broken shells. No wonder she felt so dizzy. It was the blood loss. She needed blood. Standing, she tried to check for any sign of movement. Not seeing any, she moved towards the side of the nest without any feathers, hoping the baby orik were sleeping. Holding tightly to her wound, Odesha looked over the side of the nest. The branches from the neighboring trees obscured her view, but she could make it to the ground. She could climb down the branches then make her way back towards the salt mines, heading in the general direction of where the orik flew from. Maybe there would be an animal close by she could use for blood to heal herself.

Looking back at the feathered babies sleeping silently on the side of the nest, a musky smell reached Odesha. The horrid smell made her gag before she could stop herself. She slapped a hand over her mouth to stifle the noises she was making. The babies hadn't woken up from the sounds she had inadvertently made, thankfully. An opening in the cage of branches pulled her attention away from the babies. Taking hesitant steps, she tried placing her feet in areas where there were no broken shells. If she could reach the opening, Odesha knew she had a chance to make it home.

Movement from the corner of the nest stopped her advance, one of her feet held in the air about to descend to the nest.

The mounds of feathers shifted. One of the babies facing away stood tall, fluffing the feathers behind it. The baby bird had already doubled its size after standing. She gulped, noticing they already towered over her, and realized she didn't want to wait around to see the front of it. Odesha smashed through broken shells in her haste to reach the opening in the nest.

"Oh hellfire," she cursed. It was dinner time.

When Odesha reached the opening in the side of the nest, she thrust her leg over and grabbed the closest branch, swinging her body over the side, trying not to fall to the ground. She used her hands to push off the nest. Holding her arms out, she moved slowly, while balancing to reach the trunk. Moving her feet back and forth helped her find the strong points. The tree held her weight, so she kept moving down, the wound at her side forgotten in her terror. The babies wouldn't leave their nest if she left, she hoped. Odesha swung to the next branch over and over, pushing past the pain, until a screech reached her from an adjacent nest. She hugged the dark tree she stood on, keeping silent, not wanting the birds to see her. The shadows of the feathered bundles moved quickly, the birds spreading out in waves throughout their homes above her.

Oddly, the birds moved silently for being so large; their screech was the only thing that gave them away. She continued her frantic climb down, even though her hair caught on the branches and tore from her scalp. It slowed her descent when she tried to pull free of them. Stiff branches pulled at her dress, ripping away that protection. A branch broke away from a tree when she stepped on it, falling to the ground. She looked up to see if the cracking sound was as loud as she thought. A feathered head peered over the side of the nest to confirm it was.

Unable to see the bird's face, Odesha prayed to Freyja that it hadn't spotted her. She whimpered, hugging the tree tightly. Cold breaths puffed from her mouth.

The orik sounded a warning. Its screech alerted

the others. They had found her. Odesha bared her fangs in challenge to the winged beast and continued the climb down.

They wouldn't take her down without a fight. The birds were leaving their nest when she reached the last branch on the tree, jumping down to the snow-covered ground, landing in a tight crouch. Branches snapped above her head, but she didn't look up to see what she already knew.

They were still coming.

Trying not to panic more, she tore a ribbon off her bodice to bind her side, needing to stem the flow of blood before she ran. She looked up to see how far the babies had traveled. Astonishment raced through her at the speed they moved at.

No, these were monkeys, not birds, she was sure of it.

Finding her bearings, she took off running as fast as her side would allow, but a feathered bundle dropped from a tree to block the path in front of her. Was the whole forest trying to eat her now? There wasn't enough of her to go around!

She narrowly missed the orik as she turned a different direction, her legs pumping, her feet moving so fast across the landscape they were only a blur. The pain in her side continued, making her grit her teeth in agony. She tried not to cry out, but the pain was excruciating. There were no birds around her. Their screams came from high above the trees. She dodged a giant snow tree and saw a cave in the near distance. The dark cave opened under a small hill. Get in the cave, figure out where she was, find a blood source, and make it home. She could do that, she promised herself.

At the entrance of the cave, a large rock formation grew. The rocks would protect her from view. She could hide easily among the peaks. She sprinted towards the largest rock. Odesha's body was tired and the pain in her side stabbing. But her safety came first. Turning around to face the rock, keeping her hands on the cool stone, she inched from behind her hiding place, peering into the forest. Her hands were shaking she was so scared at what she would see.

No movement could be seen through the trees. She backed up slowly, but a neighboring rock brushed against her side. A yelp of pain was wrenched from her mouth at the feeling it caused. Holding tightly to her side, she gasped, knowing something was missing. Her bandage was gone, the wound reopened. Her face lost its color when she realized…

She had left a blood trail. They would be coming.

Searching the back of the cave, she found nothing she could use to defend herself. Scooping up snow, she packed her wound tightly to stem the new blood seeping from it. If she could make it to another cave, she could get away from the trail she had left. The baby orik would think she was somewhere inside the cave and search for her there. Small pebbles littered the ground. She couldn't try to move the heavy boulders stuck in the snow. There were no weapons. She had to leave. She was an easy kill where she was.

Odesha whirled around in a flurry and bolted towards the entrance in a panic. A giant body stepped out from behind the large boulder and in her momentum, she couldn't stop. Holding her hands out to lessen the impact, it felt like she had hit a tree. The wind was knocked from her when her bottom hit the snow.

Odesha moaned in pain. A large feathered body loomed over her. More feathered birds than she could count stepped out from behind the trees. They watched her silently, their oddly shaped faces moving in a strange way. Her blinking eyes couldn't fathom the number.

A silent army waited for her in the forest for their next meal. A dull roaring sound, like a stampede, sounded in her ears. The pounding noise was getting louder. A soft puff of snow fell in front of her face, obscuring her view. Her eyes shot up to see a mass of snow ripple down from the top of the cave.

Time seemed to move slowly when the snow fell, but where could she go?

She murmured, "Avalanche," and let the snow take her.

And then…Odesha's world went dark…

CHAPTER 5

A piercing feeling cramped Odesha's stomach, waking her from her slumber. Her eyes fluttered open and she sat up gently. Wooden walls of the domain surrounded her. They were packed with ice. Shelves were full of an assortment of crude items. A wooden roof loomed over top of her.

She was in a storage room. A feather cot sat underneath her, surprisingly soft. Wooden, thick chains bound her wrists. Her injured side felt tight, wrapped with a new bandage. A rough wooden door stood in the front of the room. Her soiled, torn gown had been replaced with a short white cloth. Somebody must have undressed her and tried to heal her side, she reasoned. The feeling in her belly intensified, causing her to gasp. It twisted and turned in distress. Shoving herself over, she spewed the contents of her belly across the wooden floor. She threw up what looked like broth and small pieces of meat. She hadn't had human food in so long she had forgotten what it tasted like, but she remembered the sick feeling in her belly. The rest of the food was purged from her body. After her Reawakening, food was poison to her now, but whoever had fed her hadn't known that. After all the food was gone, her belly settled. Hunger pains for blood roared through her. The blood loss took over her needs. The faint smell of blood reached her, the copper scent wafting through her nose. The back part of the storage room came into focus, the smell coming from that direction. Hanks of meat hung from the ceiling, drying. Buckets underneath the meat caught the dripping blood to keep the floor clean.

Testing the bonds, she was able to pull the chain holding her hands together, and she moved to the bucket. Odesha let out a sigh, relieved, when she took a drink of the blood. She was careful not to spill a drop. Her body began to heal instantly from the inside out, her mind clearing of confusion, and now she was wondering where she was. The storage room didn't give any hints, so she turned her attention elsewhere. The dressing on her healed side was easy to remove even while cuffed. She tore the tight bonds away. Underneath the dressing was pale, clean skin.

Stuffing the cloth in the bottom of the bucket, she returned to her original spot on the bed. After her near-death experience, the pain from the ice circling her heart returned, freezing her. She felt almost normal again. Calm in the storm, just like at home.

A noise sounded from outside, a shuffling of feet. She sat upright, worried at who she was about to meet. A slight scrape on the door was the only warning she had before it was slammed open, bouncing against the wooden frame. The rafters rained with bits of earth and dust knocked free of their perch.

Her eyes swung upwards to see a giant…yeti…in the doorway. There was no such thing as a yeti, she tried to remind herself, blinking hard. But one was standing in front of her.

The large head bowed forward to come inside, bringing it closer for her to see it. There were many similarities between them, but he was bigger and hairier than her. Short gray hair sprouted from the yeti's head, giving him a serious, military look. The large pointed ears swiveled to lie on the side of its head as if listening for something. Its face was sharp, holding a narrow nose similar to her own. The outfit it was wearing had plates that looked like they were removed from an orik. The plates fastened around the yeti's thick neck and covered the arms and legs.

Its back had a gray feathered cape that fell to the ground. It wore a giant bone necklace, while bone piercings lined the large pointy ears.

The dark eyes studied her intensely. When it raised a hairless gray finger to her face, harsh grunts spilled from the thin mouth. Odesha's worry intensified. She knew quite a few languages, but this was something different. Maybe she should grunt back? Deciding that was a bad idea, she waited for it to do something else, continuing to stare at it blankly. She didn't speak yeti and wasn't sure if he was friendly or not. It raised a furry eyebrow. The harsh mouth tightened like it swallowed something sour. She tensed, worried he would strike out.

Oh, great Freyja, she worried. She had probably just insulted him somehow. Him?

Glancing down to its groin, her gaze quickly returned to its face, but couldn't confirm that it was a him. The plates hid his anatomy. He narrowed his eyes at her, looking annoyed.

She shrugged her shoulders helplessly and said, "I'm so sorry, I can't speak your language." The yeti's face turned shocked, the hair on its body standing on end. The large ear pivoted to hear her sounds better.

Lifting her bonds to point at herself, she stated, "Odesha".

The yeti roughly repeated back, "Oda?" It was a

good first try, but his mouth was having trouble saying her name. She tried again, repeating her name slower hoping he wouldn't become angry. Finally, after a couple tries, the yeti got it right. "Odeshhhhhhaaaaaaaaahhhhh." The syllables grunted from his mouth sounded like he had choked on his food, but at least she could understand him.

She nodded her head warily. "Yes." She pointed to herself again. "Odesha," Then pointed back to him, trying to encourage further communication. It grunted again, the harsh sound hard to decipher. Attempting a guess, she hesitated and asked, "Dek?"

The name was manly, and she prayed she had guessed his gender correctly. He nodded hard, his great bone necklace clicking together loudly with the movement.

He gestured toward the chains. Odesha raised her hands cautiously. He gripped them tightly in and broke them with his bare hands without any effort. She reevaluated her first impression of him.

He was as strong as a demon, but she would bet his bulk slowed him down. There wasn't a weapon on his side she could see. He must be harmless, she reasoned. Odesha didn't inherit many traits from her father, who was a pure demon. Her sister, Vashti, had his strength and brave spirit. All Odesha's strengths and weaknesses were inherited from her mother's side. Her speed, the curse of the ice, and her taste for blood were from the vampire side.

Dek grunted deeply and gestured towards the doorway, expecting her to follow him through it.

While Odesha tried to decipher his words, he clasped both hands to his forearms. He repeated slowly, "Odesha. Dunka ari Dek." Watching her reaction closely, Dek noticed her distress at not understanding the garbled language. The yeti repeated the gesture and phrase. Hands folding, then releasing, and a slice of his hand across the front of its throat caused her to wince. "Odesha, dunka ari Dek ro bov." Odesha nodded. She understood that.

Stay with Dek or die.

Dek stared silently at Odesha, his face serious. Reaching over slowly to not startle her, he squeezed her upper arms, testing the strength she carried. He snorted in amusement. Dek's head shook from side to side, conveying his sadness. She kept her thoughts from her face in case he could read her easily. He had decided she was weak because of her size, Odesha was sure of it. Like the demons to the south, Dek's size and strength were both intimidating, helping him survive this tough environment. She would survive here, she wasn't concerned. The ice was already inside her, it didn't matter if it was around her. Turning, Dek gestured for her to follow. Odesha stayed close to his heels and left the shed with him, hoping he would keep her safe.

Odesha looked around at her surroundings to find the way home. She kept Dek in the corner of her eye the whole time. The orik forest was behind them, far enough she could only see the shadow of the line of trees. Together they trekked towards a large wooden structure encased by ice. The structure was large, pointing high in the sky. The wooden planks were perfectly preserved in the ice. In front of the structure, a worn path through the snow had been walked frequently. On both sides of the same path, small wooden booths were set up, creating a quaint marketplace. It was crudely built, holding wares of all types. Several hanks of meat were sitting inside wooden totes covered with snow. She could see homemade cloth of fading colors. The yeti vendors were packing up their wares. They were chatting with each other in that deep grunting language that Dek had spoken. Silence permeated through the crowd when they noticed them approaching.

The other yeti resembled Dek in appearance. Their furry faces peered out for a better look. The yeti pointed and gasped at her approaching. Odesha assumed they were not used to a hairless person.

The yeti in the marketplace were dressed in light colors with loose tunics and dresses. Women yeti, being giants, lifted items easily from their stalls. Their faces had less fur and were softer in appearance. Their colors of fur differed from a light blue, white, gray, even some light browns. Different lengths of thick hair hung from each gender's head, some with plain beads woven in. They were very easy to tell apart now that there were so many in front of Odesha.

Dek's stern appearance was unique compared to others in the market, harsher, as if life had worn him down long ago. He must have had a great burden to bear. This tribe on the ice had no one to depend on but each other. That would be tough for any species. So many things could go wrong and there would be no one to turn to. They pushed forward to the large structure. Dek's powerful strides sliced through the snow. The smell of wet snow and wood swelled through the market. The ice shards dug inside Odesha's heart. It caused her to wince, and she rubbed at her chest. It was getting worse each day. In the beginning, she had tried hard to find her spark. But as the days went on, she gave up hope.

They walked around the large wooden structure,

going around the entrance. The ice had locked the structure into place for eternity.

On the other side of the structure, was a large clearing made into a circle. A raised wooden dais had been constructed on one side of the clearing. A large fire sizzled on another side. The burnt wood was the source of the smell she had experienced when first entering the marketplace. More yeti clustered in groups. They grunted and laughed with each other. A large celebration was about to occur. The yeti in the clearing were dressed in finer cloth and their hair was loose and free in the light of the fire.

Some seemed to be…missing…certain items of clothing. The nudity made Odesha avert her eyes for modesty's sake. The naked yeti did not seem to be making a stir. Instead, they blended in with the others. It would have been a riot in court if someone had dared wear such revealing outfits.

When shouting sounded off in the distance of the clearing, a small fluffy ball barreled into Odesha's healed side. Even though the ball was small, it still knocked her off balance. It didn't hurt, just scared her, so much that she cried out in alarm, alerting Dek. He turned with teeth bared, clutching a wicked-looking knife he had pulled from his back. The sharp point almost skewered Odesha while she tried to regain her balance. He was slower than she was when he moved, but much more powerful. What worried her was she hadn't seen him carrying the knife beneath the feathers. Chiding herself to be more careful, she pushed the blade to the side, nervously looking down to the bit of fluff clutching her legs. A small yeti with long brown hair and dark eyes had Odesha's legs wrapped in her twig-like arms.

Dek's eyes.

A cherub-like face, with soft hair framing its face, peered up at Odesha. It made her think the small yeti was a girl. The child smiled at Odesha with a toothy grin. Tightening her arms, the child grunted a softly worded question to Dek. Dek sighed and placed the blade back in its holster to safely hide the knife. The knife had looked to have been crafted crudely, but the bent edges and worn handle looked like they had been in many battles. But what would these people have battles with, Odesha wondered. Dek grunted a quick reply to the little one with a smile and opened his arms wide. She released Odesha's legs and jumped to wrap her arms around Dek's neck, while he nuzzled her cheek gently. Dek's show of affection surprised Odesha. He had seemed so stern around her that she had thought he would be the same around his children. His large hairy arm gestured to Odesha and the girl to introduce the two.

"Odesha, Dede."

Odesha nodded her head in understanding. She whispered, in vampire tongue, "Dede, very pleased to meet you." The lyrical sounds of her voice were pleasing compared to demonish. If she continued to whisper, she thought it would help show Dek she was meek and not aggressive.

Dede looked confused at the foreign tongue, scrunching her face prettily to grunt a question to Dek. After shaking his head in response to her question, Dede shrugged and climbed down his body to hold out her hand to Odesha patiently.

Odesha glanced at Dek, worried to touch the child. He stared back at her in grave warning, tilting his head to the side, waiting to see what she would do in response. Odesha translated that look with a gulp. He was warning her, if she harmed his child it would be a horrible fate and he could easily do it with that sharp blade. Not wanting to test his patience, she placed her hand over her heart and bowed her head to let him know she wasn't a threat.

Not yet, at least.

Dek looked suspicious at first. His body gradually relaxed when he recognized her sincerity. With a sigh, he turned around to walk closer to the fire. Occasionally, he would glance back and watch them walking hand in hand with a thoughtful look. It was a good start.

CHAPTER 6

The fire was a beautiful backdrop to the ice surrounding the group. The dancing reflection carried across the snow, casting shadows. The large full moon shined brightly, giving the air an unearthly glow. It was a winter wonderland full of beings she never knew existed. But she wished her family was here. Vashti would've loved to join the celebration, Saphira would've loved to explore the new environment, and Endemion would've been looking for the tribe's weakness to use against them. Father would've been drinking along with the groups, making merry as always. The thought of her lost family caused Odesha to shiver as the icy cold continued to batter her failing heart, insidious in its pursuit to overtake her. It was getting harder to move her extremities. Like a great weight had settled on her. But at least she would have the memories of her family in her last moments.

The tribe of yeti was larger than Odesha previously had thought. Unable to count their numbers, many groups were clustered around a large charred animal being roasted on a spit. Easily big enough to feed these numbers, people rotated to give others a break at turning. It took a lot of strength to push the heavy animal. Odesha squinted, trying to identify what they were cooking, but it was so badly mangled and cooked she couldn't. The smell of blood was mouthwatering. The meat smell, not so much. She still remembered the taste of the broth from earlier. She grimaced, smacking her lips, not wanting to go through that again.

Many yeti looked to be teenagers. They danced around each other to the beat of drums played by several older yeti. They were showing off for the crowd. Their moves were boisterous and coordinated. Odesha could tell they had been practicing for a long time together. The yeti that watched, cheered them on, clapping loudly and yelling encouragement. She wasn't used to this type of celebration. The ones at Merdi were calm and controlled, until the king had too much to drink. At that point, Odesha would retire to her room to let others coral him, usually Endemion.

There were many children participating in the celebration, unlike Merdi where children stayed at home with servants. Dede noticed a group of children playing with a ball covered with animal hide and started to fidget. She released Odesha's hand to join them as they kicked the ball around and screamed in happiness. Odesha tapped Dek on the arm, gesturing to Dede playing to let him know where she was going, so he didn't think she ate the poor child. He looked to where she pointed at and nodded his head. He must be used to Dede running away, Odesha reasoned.

Suddenly, a yeti tribe member broke away from one of the larger groups on the other side of the circle and sprinted towards Dek with arms wide. Odesha's jaw fell open when she noticed the large yeti had only a band of cloth around her swinging breasts and a loincloth to cover her very large derriere. The cloth was unable to hold her size, bouncing from side to side, showing everyone her assets. Odesha's face heated, her hand slapping across her forehead. She just wasn't used to this much nudity around her, but she was trying not to offend by her stares and opinions, hurriedly putting her hand down.

This yeti was one of the shortest adult yeti she had seen, but was still larger than Odesha. Her gray hair hung in giant waves to just below her shoulders.

The screaming grunts pulled attention from the crowd to the approaching Dek. Cheers and raised clay bowls began like a ripple from the crowd of yeti. The female yeti was a bouncy whirlwind of chaos. Odesha wanted to shield her eyes to give her privacy, but she worried if that may have been another insult. The tribe around Odesha was taking it in stride. The two embraced in a tangle of limbs. Dek dipped her down low to the ground, making the female laugh in joy. They rubbed noses together and smiled at each other, oblivious to the scene they were creating. How odd. Do they not kiss? Odesha had seen courtiers engaged in affairs in the castle's halls, watching them moan in enjoyment of each other. Their mouths clung to each other with passion, making her burn in sadness to never experience what they felt. Odesha had always walked away feeling lonelier than she had been before. This open affection was refreshing. The joy and happiness felt contagious. Sighing, feeling sad, she would have liked to experience this kind of happiness one day, but that wasn't in her future.

Dek grunted and pulled his female upright. They clasped hands and walked towards the circle of yeti she had just left, talking back and forth in their language. Dek forgot about his captive so quickly, Odesha realized the new yeti must be his fire. The thaw to a heart caused from a spark, as mother used to say. The one thing that could save her, now. Or kill, just like her mother.

Odesha sighed and looked down at a slab of ice at her feet, seeing her rough appearance reflected. The blood she had drunk earlier made her lips turn a dark red. Her straight white hair lay in disarray. She ran her fingers through the tresses to fix the worst snarls. Her long, slim legs shone brightly in the moonlight. The crown she once wore was gone, reminding her she wasn't a princess there, just a regular person trying to fit in where she didn't belong. The loose, pale dress barely covered her bottom, so she tugged on it uncomfortably. It must've been made for a child since the female yeti's garb would swallow her whole, hanging from her thin frame. At least being frozen she couldn't feel the cold. Alarmed, she reached for her chest and gasped. Where was the necklace? Odesha let out a breath of air when she felt it nestled protectively between her breasts. The yeti hadn't removed it.

That could have been disastrous if they had taken it, not knowing what it was for. If Vashti had been summoned, the yeti would have killed her in their fright. Of course, Dek happened to turn around when he realized Odesha wasn't following him. He noticed her own breasts in her hands, his raised brow said as much. Odesha felt a blush cross her face in her embarrassment, calmly lowered her arms down to her side, trying to look confident. Dek rolled his eyes and grunted a question. She walked closer to hear him, her head tilted in confusion.

He gestured to the woman to introduce the two. "Odesha, Fanni." Odesha froze when she realized what he said. She tried to keep her composure over the apt name.

Odesha executed a deep curtsy reserved for visiting queens in Merdi, keeping a straight face and replied, "Greetings, Miss Fanni."

Fanni puckered her large mouth and made several attempts to say Odesha's name. It only caused a slight wince before she got it right. Being this close to the female, Odesha noticed her striking eyes. They were a light blue like the ice around them. When Fanni said her name correctly, Odesha nodded her head with an attempt to smile. It felt brittle, her lips almost cracking. She had watched the groups around smiling, so she knew it wouldn't be taken as aggression. They showed happiness and affection just like her own people. Except for kisses. Odesha hadn't seen one yet, even to the children. Dek waved Odesha forward arrogantly, pleased that she was so well behaved. Odesha stood beside Fanni while they walked together. Fanni grunted and gestured at the yeti they passed, who continued to stare with bewilderment at their odd group. Nodding her head, keeping her facial expression serene, Odesha's insides felt like they were in turmoil, unsure if Fanni was trying to introduce her to the tribe or if she was telling them to stay away. Her lack of facial and body hair must be horrifying for these people to look at. But if they only knew what she really was. A monster that lived off blood. That would be even worse.

They reached the innermost circle of almost naked people. The flames of the fire put off so much heat it reminded Odesha of the heat dungeon she took Vladeric to. Her low hiss alerted Fanni, who turned with concern to view Odesha. She tugged at Odesha's gown and clucked her tongue like a chicken. That's why they were almost naked; it was like hellfire the heat was so intense.

Odesha shrugged her shoulders. She motioned towards a large ice cap she had spotted in the near distance to Fanni. She didn't have anything else to wear, so she would just have to stay away from the fire. It was close enough to see and be a part of the celebration, but far enough she wouldn't be uncomfortable. Fanni gestured and nodded enthusiastically. A sharp tug to Dek's fur called his attention to her. They grunted back and forth to each other, arguing about what the best choice would be.

Keep the furless creature close, or far away enough she could run, Odesha silently translated. She wasn't sure if that's what they were saying, but she still attempted to understand. A decision must have been reached between the two, because Dek turned toward Odesha and nodded his head, signaling she could stay on her ice cap.

He gestured to the far ice in the distance, the darkness terrifying in its stillness, and grunted, "Bov."

Death. But because nothing could survive in the darkness or because he would hunt her down? Odesha didn't want to find out. Deciding to stay close, she bowed her head. Her soft steps took her to the spot she chose.

If the yeti had been cruel to her, she would've killed them by now. They had been so kind she wasn't sure what to think. Were they civilized or did they just live simply? The curiosity about the tribe was the reason she hadn't fled yet, Odesha reasoned. Not to mention the blood supply. She would need a lot to reach Antiqua, not able to survive the ice without nourishment. She sat down and tucked her short skirt to the side to get comfortable on her new perch. Dede ran by her while kicking her ball. The small child laughed happily, waving to her. The laughter and gaiety of the people were infectious.

Dek and Fanni seemed to be in a hearty discussion with an elderly yeti. Odesha studied their body language. Most people bowed their heads to Dek. It showed her he had a place of high importance in the group, a chieftain of this tribe. He commanded respect and many came to speak with him. She studied the tribe closer and learned the dynamics and the social structure, but the language barrier made it hard.

Dede distracted her again, almost tripping over her own feet. She reminded Odesha so much of Evie, it hurt. There was no way to know if Evie had survived the orik attack. While she watched the children play with the ball, fighting over whose turn it was, Dede decided to take her turn and kicked the ball too hard. It landed on the back of a naked yeti, her privates only covered by a hanging blue triangular cloth. The liquid spilled from her cup onto her arm after the ball smacked her. Her long, dark gray hair was littered with large beads. The naked yeti turned to Dede, after she righted herself. She yelled in admonishment, the anger clear on her face. Dede instantly began sobbing, her small shoulders shaking in distress at being yelled at by the older yeti, unable to even choke out an apology.

Dek noticed the commotion and shouted, "Sashi!" The yelled word must be the new yeti's name. Not a favored one of Dek's then. Odesha gripped her knees tightly, worried that the young yeti would retaliate on Dede and worried what her own reaction would be if she did attack. The little girl had found a place inside her heart somehow. Maybe it was Dede's innocence or the way she gave her that small hug when she didn't even know her, but something inside of Odesha wanted to protect that little girl.

Sashi rolled her eyes at Dek. She sipped at her cup, not caring that Dede was crying at her feet still, when she caught sight of Odesha on the ice cap watching the spectacle. Sashi's eyes traveled down Odesha's body. She turned her nose up, sneering, clearly dismissing Odesha's presence. Brother would've had her tongue removed if Sashi had dismissed a princess like that in court, but Odesha reined in her temper at the clear dismissal. Seeing Dede trying to wipe her own tears while she tried to run after her friends turned Odesha's stomach. Dede was a resilient little yeti, Odesha would give her that much. Sashi must be of high importance in this group to assume she could yell at Dek's daughter. She would have to watch her step around that one.

Another yeti stood by Sashi, not getting involved with either side in the conflict. The way she stood, hunched over, trying to shield herself from being noticed, caught Odesha's attention. This yeti had light blue fur on her body. It softly framed her face. Her light brown eyes watched the spectacle carefully. Her shyness was apparent when she bowed to Dek in respect. Dek seemed to like this yeti more when he smiled at her. So, it was just Sashi he didn't like. Some members of the tribe began to approach Odesha under the watchful eye of Fanni, but when they tried to touch her hairless legs or face, Fanni pointed them away. Odesha tried to keep calm, giving the yeti a blank expression when they attempted to speak. She shook her head or kept her eyes downcast, unsure of how to tell them she couldn't understand besides a light shrug. The yeti lost interest when she showed no reaction to them.

Odesha turned her attention to the fire. The flames crawled up the trees the yeti had gathered from the orik forest. She hadn't been around a fire in a long time, having stayed in the castle. Floating around the castle with no purpose, she was just a paperweight taking up space, until the salt mines. Father was determined to figure out where the profits were going. It was her job to find out the cause and deliver punishment. Odesha was determined to help Antiqua before she joined the gardens, and to find a way back home. The guards would surely be searching around the mountainside for her, but she had seen the distance the orik had traveled. They wouldn't be able to reach her. She would find a way to get past the orik forest and help her people, even if Gamble was hiding the truth from her, but she couldn't see the sweet man taking the money for himself.

A rough group of men talked with each other around the animal that had been cooked, while others cut pieces of the meat, distributing them among the people on clay plates. Many young tribe women tried getting the men's attention. They helped to supply the plates, sharing a word or two with the men. At the men's backs were thick capes coated with feathers like what Dek was wearing. Odesha was positive they contained hidden weapons as well. Scarred metal plates adorned their body in different shapes. Their size was comparable to Dek's, their presence foreboding and strong as their muscles rippled in the firelight. Some had long hair twisted in intricate knots, others short hair. Their colors came in a variety. Gray, blue, and brown sprinkled throughout, but there was one difference that set them apart.

These men were warriors. Hunters, whispered through her mind. They must have killed this beast to feed their people. Taking a deep breath, a memory filtered through her mind. The musky smell entered her nose, reminding her of the smell from the orik nests. It was hard to forget. The only thing these men were missing was the decorated feathered head. Odesha tugged on Fanni's hand, who was still standing next to her after dismissing another yeti trying to speak with her, to get her attention. Odesha had been so distracted she hadn't noticed.

When Fanni turned with a questioning look, Odesha pointed towards the men and flapped her arms slightly like a bird, lifting her shoulders questioningly. She wanted to know what those men had to do with the orik.

Fanni glanced toward the men and pointed toward the animal on the spit, bringing her fingers together. So, the food was becoming scarce here.

Fanni flapped her arms. She brought her arms together and ran in front of Odesha pretending to drop the nonexistent burden she carried. The orik dropped the prey. Fanni hid her face. She jumped up suddenly and pretended to grab something off the ground, running in place, her hand miming eating

"Bulvo," Fanni stated. She grabbed at her back and pretended to sword fight. Bulvo meant hunter. The hunters were tasked with retrieving the prey for the tribe. The responsibility must fall hard on their shoulders, especially if their food source was dwindling. No wonder Dek looked so tired. Odesha nodded her head, understanding. She had been halfway right after all. The orik brought food to their young, the yeti took the food from the nest. These people were close to starvation if they couldn't find any game on the ice and had to venture into the orik's nest.

With the dangers of the orik forest, the tribe wouldn't be able to cross into Antiqua. Looking at these people in a new light, she could see why they celebrated this feast. This had to be rare to have this amount of food. Cooking and preserving it would be their best option, but they still had to feed their people first. She thought it had been strange the baby orik were following her from their safe nests, but now she realized the feathered bundles weren't orik. The yeti were trying to save her, to bring her here to the tribe. Odesha just couldn't understand their language enough to thank them. Her heart swelled with gratitude and she placed her hand over her heart. Odesha nodded to Fanni, trying to tell her she knew what they did for her. Fanni smiled enthusiastically, rushing off when Dek called her name. Odesha had much to think about. Her premature assumptions had been unfounded, but she would keep learning from the mistakes she made.

Hearing a loud cough, Odesha turned around to find a disheveled hunter on his knees in front of her.

He was eye level with her he was so tall, holding a clay plate gently. A large slab of meat was on top of it in offering to her. Shorter than Dek, with light blue fur, his face looked thoughtful as if he was trying to figure her out. He wasn't intimidating with his blue-eyed stare, thankfully. He was calm and being patient with her. She hadn't had the chance to speak with a hunter yet and wanted this chance now.

Pushing the plate towards Odesha, he grunted, "Yemi." He mimed eating with his clawed hand, while his long ears rotated to hear her reply. Yemi meant eat. He could be one of her rescuers and she didn't want to offend him. She placed her hand over her heart and nodded her head to show her thanks, staring into his eyes, showing him her seriousness, and reached for the plate slowly to not scare him away.

"Boni," he grunted out. Odesha blinked her eyes trying to recognize the word. It was close to Bulvo, but he had said it slightly different.

"Boni?"

He nodded his head, gestured to himself, and repeated, "Boni." He pointed back to her and waited for her name.

"Odesha."

This took a bit for Boni to say, but when he did, she nodded in approval and showed him her strained smile. Boni stared at her longer, the curiosity shining bright in his eyes. What was he looking for? Deciding to try a new word she'd learned to break the tension, she cleared her throat and said, "Boni, bulvo?"

She tried to string words together to learn their language faster. The grunting part she was still perfecting but it sounded better with each try. He seemed startled at her use of his language, but he reached to his hidden sword under his cape anyway, nodded his head, and brought it forth for her to admire. It was long and made dully, as if crafted with a crude weapon, but the end was sharp. The handle was made of animal hide and thick cloth tied together.

He turned slightly to the animal roasting, pointing to the large group of large males she had noticed earlier and grunted, "Bulvo."

She heard a soft whistle in the distance, and it startled him so much he almost fell over. Before she could reach out and catch him, he stood quickly and ran off toward the sound without another word.

Odesha glanced around to see if anyone else was watching the strange encounter and noticed Sashi and her friend staring at her. When Odesha looked at Sashi's friend, she looked miserable. What had caused that reaction? She watched the interaction between the two, trying to figure out their words and gestures, but still couldn't understand. Boni made it back to the large group of men. Sashi's friend's eyes were trained on him the entire way. He leaned in to speak with someone in the back of the group she couldn't see. Odesha tried shifting her body to get a better angle when the crowd parted.

And Odesha noticed him.

The tallest yeti she had seen yet stood watching her on the other side of the fire. His aqua eyes stared straight into her own. They burned with an inner heat. His body, sculpted with hard, lean muscles, made her want to bite each area to mark her territory. Bite? Great Freyja, she had never wanted to bite someone before. Boni stood on tiptoes to speak in his ear. A giant yeti among the ice. This was the hunter.

And the queen's frozen heart sparked with life.

The hunter's golden locks threaded with white were braided down to the middle of his back, free of beads. His feathered cape flowed behind him in the breeze, while his scarred front plates glimmered in the firelight. Odesha's eyes kept holding his as her chest thumped with the beating of her heart. White hair swirled in the hollows of his chiseled face. It made her have the urge to feel the texture. She slowly licked her lips, drawing his hard gaze to her mouth. Somehow his expression turned even more carnal and her insides clenched in response. Her hands on the clay plate began to shake. She tried to hold it more tightly so he wouldn't notice her reaction. The hunter's gaze traveled down her body, seeing the uneaten meat in her hands. The sharp eyes cleared of lust and slid to Boni. While he talked to Boni, she continued to stare at his strong, sharp teeth like a lovesick fool.

Fool! That's what she was. Remember mother's warning, she scolded herself. Or she would fall like her. To her own death. Several females giggling broke her from the trance she was in. Odesha tore her gaze away. Her vampire half was coming out as her mind screamed at her to sink her claws in and mark him, but that was impossible. She couldn't be fated for a yeti… Right?

Kunchok had ordered Boni to bring meat to the pale creature he had hunted in the forest. Boni hadn't questioned him, Kunchok's word was law and Boni hoped to gain favor with the lead hunter. Boni had reported the creature was smart, learning their words quickly. The kindness she showed had surprised Boni, reporting that finding with a smile. Kunchok had been intrigued with her since he had first seen her, running swiftly through the mangled trees. Her scent had about taken him to his knees, the fresh smell causing his heart to beat wildly, something he had never felt before. It surprised him the cold didn't bother her since she didn't have fur like his people. He would watch her closely to make sure she wouldn't a threat. To him or his people. The gathering had made him cross. He had warned Dek that they couldn't afford to keep eating large portions of the meat the hunters gathered. There wasn't enough food and it was Kunchok's job as lead hunter to provide. He had to work twice as hard to keep the stores full. Dek's excuse was the tribe needed to celebrate or tensions would increase and the council would become involved. Kunchok wanted to see them get involved, he dared them to. He wasn't in the mood to deal with their politics.

CHAPTER 7

*O*desha ducked her head in distress to hide her face. The lust in her eyes would easily give her away. They shined like diamonds casting out a beacon in the darkness. Strong emotions caused the iris to change, glinting like silver shards. Odesha prayed the firelight hid them. That he thought it was just a trick of light. Distracted in her own thoughts, she missed the danger approaching behind. The smells were diminished from her senses, the low footsteps approaching were all secondary to her own turbulent thoughts. The childlike screams filtered through her ears. It took her back to the terror she felt the day she tried to save Evie. She almost thought she was back in Antiqua reliving the horror, but the fire continued to burn brightly in front of her. She shook herself out of her surprise, knowing she was still on the other side of the mountain.

Something else was coming.

A furred, giant beast sprinted towards the group of children Dede had been playing with.

It resembled the cows seen grazing on the open hillsides in Merdi, but the sharp tusks stood taller than its snout. The unseeing white eyes rolled in its head. Small tracks of blood flowed from the corner of its eyes, creating a sinister appearance. White foam poured from its mouth. The sick bull charged towards its prey. A loud war cry boomed, making her shiver in its intensity.

The hunter raced toward the children, but he wouldn't make it in time. The children would fall to those giant hooves first; they were on the end of the clearing leaving their forgotten ball behind. They scrambled to reach safety, their small feet tripping over themselves in the snow. One of them caught her eye—Dede! She struggled against the snow to reach safety, but she had been the one retrieving the ball she had kicked too far.

Dek and the hunters rushed towards the children, weapons drawn, but they were no match for the great beast's stampede. Odesha had ended up in the wrong place, but maybe it was for the best. She could save Dede from a horrible death, but she couldn't save them all unless…

Odesha braced herself, knowing her decision to interfere could change their fate and hers. It could mean her own death when they found out what she could do. But there was no hesitation in her choice.

Odesha's mind was decided. Holding her hand outstretched, fangs extended, nails sharp, she called forth the magic. She felt the power she had neglected slither through her. Its icy balm soothed her. When she recognized the ice and pushed it outward, shaping what she wanted to create, her breath fogged, her mind cleared. Odesha formed a spear of ice, sharp and deadly in the firelight. She had thought in the beginning if she quit using the magic it would fade from her heart, but it never did. It grew. Sprinting with untraceable speed, she raced forward to place herself between the beast and the children. Crouching in front of the group of children that clung to each other in fear, she kept her eye on the beast barreling down with all its strength towards them. The giant hooves shook the snow. Its rotten stench was overpowering, as the breath burst from its frothing mouth. Odesha flashed her fangs at the beast in challenge. She wouldn't fall here, that wasn't her destiny. Her life was her own and she had a choice. Odesha adjusted her aim, pulling her arm back to prepare her throw and let loose a war cry, channeling all her strength to hit her target.

The spear sliced through the air and crashed through the eye of the beast. The beast gave a great bellow, the horrid stink of death leaving its mouth. It threw its large head back, the earth shuddering when it crashed on its side. The body slid across the snow coming to rest close to Odesha. Its tongue hung from its mouth and with one last exhale, the beast's life was over. The silence of the yeti seemed to last ages, when it only lasted seconds, while they processed what happened. The children whimpered in shock, eyes wide, and mouths even wider. They stared at Odesha standing bravely in front of them shielding them from the monster. The speed she had moved was only a blink of the eye to them. They were astonished at the strength in this stranger. A stranger that was smaller and more delicate looking than them.

The group of adult yeti closest to the children finally reached them. They screamed in terror at the near loss, frightened at what they would find. Parents and children embraced, and the hunters circled the fallen beast to check to make sure it was dead. The beast was enormous. Long hanks of fur covered its body. It was made to survive in the deep ice in the coldest weather. This may be what the tribe had hunted before they started going to the orik nests, before food became scarce. Dek scooped Dede up tightly. Fanni fell to her knees, embracing Dek's legs, crying. They were overwhelmed with terror. They had almost lost their only child. Odesha had a sudden feeling of pain while standing there watching everyone have their reunion and celebrate their life. She had no one to celebrate with. Here or Antiqua. Maybe being frozen alone was more painful than what the fire could bring, she mused.

In front of the fallen beast, stood the hunter that had caught her eye earlier. He took charge of the other men and growled orders. He led the tribe, while Dek continued to be distracted with the brush of death his family had experienced. The hunter's large ears swiveled to check for more hidden threats. Not finding any, he moved to check on the families that embraced their small children tightly to their chests. He cared for the people, that much was obvious. And the people cared for him. The children felt safe with him around them, their tears clearing from their faces when they saw he was near.

Odesha didn't think the yeti had seen her grow the weapon. They had been scrambling to reach the children. She hoped that the tribe thought the icicle had been pulled from a branch or the ice cap she had been sitting on. Before the ice had made its way to her heart, she had enjoyed throwing spears at targets with Vashti. Instead of the bow that Saphira wielded, Odesha wielded the ice. She never ran out and always hit her mark because the ice was an extension of herself. But the pain in her heart made her stop using it.

After the commotion quieted, Dek walked up to Odesha. He held a solemn Dede. His large hand landed a firm pat on Odesha's back that made her grunt in discomfort. Dek didn't know his own strength. He whispered, "Lisha vo. Lisha vo."

Lisha vo. Thank you.

The emotion on his face was plain to read. The small tears that fell from his large dark eyes made her nod speechlessly. Fanni stood to wrap her arms around Odesha. She squeezed Odesha between her giant breasts. Odesha tried to gain her breath in great gulps.

Can't breathe!

She patted Fanni on the back with a free hand to communicate her distress. Fanni began to cry again when she noticed the beast was still on its side in the snow staring sightlessly towards their group. She struggled to contain her emotions and hiccupped her distress. Dek clutched his family close, Odesha crushed in between. He held up one arm and yelled, "Densho! Densho!"

The silence of the people gave Odesha another word to add to her ever-growing list.

Densho. Silence.

Dek made a long, drawn-out speech, full of loud barked words, to the shocked crowd gathered. He thumped his chest hard, causing his plates to vibrate. It created a loud gong-like sound. The yeti all raised one hand in a unanimous cheer. They agreed with Dek, celebrating his decision. Wishing she could understand, Odesha nodded her head in support, hoping she hadn't just agreed to her death like a fool.

Everyone was jubilant. Except the hunter. He was silent. He stood up from comforting one of the children, his aqua eyes swirling with emotion as they held fast to hers. The hunter's hands clenched hard at his sides. Odesha was unsure how to read his face, his mood foreign to her. Was he angry with her? Happy?

The party resumed and no one took her away to her death. The yeti gave toasts and cheers rang out. The merriment raged through the large group. Extra sentries were posted around the celebration in case other beasts came. The yeti did not want to be caught unaware again. Hunters took the cow beast towards the shed to cut and store the meat. Odesha sat back down on the ice cap. An assortment of yeti brought Odesha things she might need. Meat, a clay cup to drink from, and a cloth to place around her shoulders. She placed the offerings on the ground, clapping along to the people singing and dancing. Occasionally, someone came and filled Odesha's clay chalice that she poured into the snow when no one was looking. The meat was taken away uneaten.

She joined in their fun from her perch, trying to fight her growing discomfort. The ice shards pierced her heart in retribution for using their power. It was excruciating in its anger to punish her. The pain dulled the roar of the crowd while Odesha massaged her chest absently. A feather-light touch on her back made her turn with a greeting, until she realized who it was.

The crowd faded into the background. Her smile froze in shock. The hunter. With his arms crossed, his eyes remained locked on Odesha. Her lungs protested when she resisted to take a deep breath. She feared his scent would be her undoing. She would bite him and never let go. The fire would consume her.

And she would be lost. If they were parted when she left, she would die. Odesha stood slowly. The hunter's nostrils flared, and his eyes narrowed when she curtsied deeply and bowed her head in respect. She felt him catch her chin in hand to pull her gaze upwards. Her face was starting to turn red from lack of oxygen and her head was becoming dizzy.

He grunted, "Vo lo cos suti ba suta." The unfamiliar words rang in her head on repeat. The hunter's aqua gaze and her silver eyes clashed. She didn't know what he just said, but whatever it was, he truly meant it.

Dek called out loudly, "Kunchok!" It drew the hunter's attention away from her. Dek motioned for the large hunter to come to him with a smile.

His name was Kunchok.

The name whispered through her mind as if it would seal inside her forever. Kunchok released Odesha with a growl of anger. He gave her one last blazing look and walked towards Dek. He obviously wanted to stay, but the chief had issued an order. She took a deep breath in relief and regretted it. The lingering scent of him was mouthwatering, but she tried to shake the fogginess from her brain.

Odesha whispered, "Dunka ari." She wanted the impossible. To stay with him too.

Dek and Kunchok embraced as they walked up the raised platform together to sit on the dais. Dek's central chair proclaimed him as chief. It was littered with bones and feathers fastened together with hide. The hunter's chair on Dek's right had black snow trees bent together to proclaim him lead hunter. The way the throne was crafted would take great strength and skill. A small feathered chair sat on the left for Fanni. She was still bouncing from group to group, Dede still firmly at her side. She wasn't going to let her wander off for a long time.

The hunter watched Odesha during the night. He only turned away when his fellow hunters or Dek talked with him. He seemed reluctant to pull his attention away from her, but when he did, it gave Odesha a chance to study him.

He was good with his people, and he had a kind voice for a grunting yeti and his smile lit up the dais. When the tribe smiled back in return, Odesha wished she could understand what he said to them. But she had learned a lot as a voyeur in the halls of Merdi and could tell when a person was uncomfortable just by studying body language.

Kunchok kept Odesha in his sight when he had no one to talk to, afraid she would disappear. She tried to ignore the attention Kunchok showed her, not wanting to encourage him, but it was increasingly difficult. She wanted to get to know him, but the stakes were too high. The pull was so strong to go up to the dais, to be around him. If only they spoke a language that they could both understand, so she could explain. The people at her castle knew to stay away from her, had always given her a wide berth because of the ice. Some whispered it was catching, others whispered why bother making friends when she would join the garden, and others felt pity for her. This hunter tried to break down her walls with a simple look. It was something she was unaccustomed to.

The music died down late at night. The mood of the yeti changed. A soft tension ran through them, different from the moods before.

Fanni motioned for a woman to come take Dede away when the poor child yawned loudly. Dede waved to Odesha on her ice cap. Odesha waved back to the charming child to bid her a silent good night. Dek stepped up to the front of the raised dais, arms outstretched. A horn sounded from the musicians and the crowd quieted to a low murmur. The crowd formed a circle in the middle of the clearing, the fire still flaming high, giving the yeti a glow. Looking around, everyone remaining at the celebration had gathered together. They stood around expectantly, waiting for something.

Dek yelled to the crowd, "Densho! Densho!"

The talking stopped. The yeti were silent, when a slow thump of the drum sounded. Odesha looked up to Kunchok, wondering what he was thinking, but his attention was solely on her. Not on what Dek or the tribe was doing. She blushed in response. His arms stayed braced on his throne, his large muscles flexed in the firelight, making her mouth dry up. The sudden urge to run to him, to throw herself in his arms and never let go gripped her. The golden hair called for her to run her fingers through it. But the need for caution, for self-preservation was forefront in her mind. A noise from the crowd pulled her attention back to the circle.

A female yeti walked to the middle of the circle. She had started to dance. Her beaded hair and short dress moved to the music. Her long arms and legs twisted in her slow dance in perfect symphony. The yeti's size prevented it from being seductive, but a sensual grace was portrayed by the story she weaved. The dance moved her to a group of hunters standing silently in the circle. They watched her move towards them and many grinned in response. The dancer reached out into the crowd, not missing a beat, and grabbed a male yeti who turned his head to smile in triumph at his friends that he left behind. He was a short yeti with dark gray skin and hair. The female danced and twirled around the male, who followed her with his eyes. It seemed to be just them in their own world, drawing closer to one another in the world the dancer had created. The air around them became heavy with anticipation. The yeti in the circle whispered to one another. They smiled together with a hidden secret, like they knew what would happen between the two. Another female came out of the crowd and took up the dance. Her dance was fierce, harder compared to the other. She sliced through the air and spun around the male. He looked astonished as he glanced back and forth between the females. The dancer continued to spin and weave, creating a chaotic whirlwind as the drums beat louder and louder.

The dancers stopped. The drums ceased their song.

The dancers stood side by side, facing the male hunter, breathing heavily. The crowd was silence, tense, waiting for something. The male hunter in the circle looked back and forth between the females, his gaze hesitant as he made his decision. He marched forward, reached out to the first female dancer, and swung her into his arms. He nuzzled her neck happily. The crowd erupted in cheers. Odesha looked up to Kunchok, his eyes at half-mast as he watched the spectacle, his body tense. What was he thinking of? She tried to picture what he would've done if she would've danced for him. And it scared her to think what she would've done.

She would never let him go.

The second dancer's face looked happy for the couple. She stepped back to her place among the crowd with a smile on her face. The drums began their beat for the second time. Kunchok moved his gaze to Odesha. His eyes blazed with heat and instantly she felt trapped, unable to move. Out of the corner of her eye, Odesha vaguely noticed a new woman stepped to the middle of the circle. She nervously danced, but Odesha was unable to tear her gaze from Kunchok to watch. What did he want from her with that look? Dek turned Kunchok's attention with a hand motion toward the circle, breaking the unspoken conversation they seemed to be having more frequently. She was falling for a yeti that she couldn't speak to. It was dangerous for her. Odesha turned away, realizing it just wasn't meant to be.

The ceremony continued late into the dark night.

With the last boom of the drums and several couples later, Odesha had figured out the point of the ceremony. This was their bonding ceremony. The females chose the male, bringing him in the circle to show him her dance, but the male made the final decision on who his mate would be. The yeti dispersed through the clearing back to their homes. Fanni took Odesha's hand. She pulled her up to stand. Odesha looked back to the throne to take a final look at Kunchok, but his seat was empty. An empty sadness ripped through Odesha. It startled her, this emotion she kept feeling for him that she tried to ignore. The ice strengthened around her heart. For once, she was grateful for it. That was the only thing that helped her walk away from him.

Fanni and Odesha walked towards the frozen structure Odesha had passed with Dek after leaving the meat shed. The empty marketplace they passed was eerie in the moonlight. Odesha peered out in the night, noticing what she missed before. Small wooden huts encrusted with ice circled the larger wooden structure. The tribe dispersed to their homes to rest for another day. The doorway of the large wooden keep loomed ahead. Fanni indicated for Odesha to go through the doorway first. Walking along the aged wood hall, they passed many open vacant rooms. It was oddly familiar, the way the rooms were set up.

Fanni motioned to one of the central rooms and grunted, "Dek and Fanni." She hesitated before a smaller room and whispered, "Dede." The far end of the hall held a doorway that Fanni motioned towards she nodded. "Odesha." The room was in shouting distance, but far enough for privacy. Odesha was thankful she got her own room, instead of chains.

Odesha nodded her head and bowed to Fanni, but Fanni's bouncing steps had already moved on. Smiling, she shook her head and pushed aside the animal hide. A simple bed made of gray feathers and dark wood sat inside. Fanni appeared again with an armload of clothing. This tribe didn't have to be kind to her even if Odesha had saved some. She was grateful they were giving her so much.

"Lisha vo," Odesha whispered quietly to Fanni, gesturing around her. She gently touched the soft fabric. Fanni turned in astonishment to Odesha. She almost knocked her down in the small room in her rush. Her mouth opened and closed like a fish.

Fanni grunted, "Vo Riwa." She placed her hands together at her head to mime sleep.

"You sleep," Fanni had said. After this long day Odesha believed she could sleep. Maybe without the nightmares of the ice garden this time.

Fanni's great strides took up the distance between them to crush Odesha in a giant hug. She grunted emotionally, "Lisha vo. Lisha vo."

Odesha patted her on her rather soft, naked back, unable to speak in the tight clasp. Fanni released her abruptly and left the room. Odesha took in large gasping breaths. She tried to recover and wondered if she would ever get used to that.

Odesha turned to the bedside table, a cloth and a bowl of fresh snow ready for her to freshen up before bed. Inside her heart, she was worried that she was coming to care for this tribe of yeti that she would soon have to leave behind.

CHAPTER 8

A feeling of being watched during the night woke her up from a light sleep. She hadn't been asleep long, unable to stop her thoughts that raced through her mind. Her eyes fluttered open to search her room. Kunchok stood poised in her doorway, holding the hide to the side. He must have only recently arrived because he was speaking with Dek, who was still yawning. She watched them talk back and forth, gesturing in a certain direction. Dek finally nodded, moving back towards his room to leave Kunchok alone with her. She sat up, alarmed.

Kunchok reared back, surprised she had woken so easily. He held up his hands to show her he meant no harm. But what was he doing in her room at night? She pulled the cover up and watched him warily.

He sat on the only chair in her room, taking a deep breath to explain what he was doing there, but it wasn't going to be easy since she didn't understand the language. He started out pointing towards Odesha, then pointed to himself, but hesitated, pointing towards a far wall. His long fingers moved up and down on the open palm of his other hand miming walking. He wanted her to go for a walk with him? She nodded her head, more at ease. All she had was unpleasant thoughts to help her fall asleep. A walk would keep her mind occupied.

Kunchok's held out his hand to help her up from the larger bed, sending small needles of feeling through her fingertips, making them tingle. When she pulled the cover away to swing her legs to the side, the tunic she wore moved up, showing quite a bit of her exposed leg. He gasped and turned to keep his eyes averted from the sight. Why was he so shy around her? The yeti were more exposed at the gathering she had been to.

Odesha adjusted the tunic and grasped his hand to make him look at her again. He turned back around when she pulled up from the bed, but continued to hold her hand. His scent was masked with the musky scent of an orik. He must have put the secreted smell harvested from the baby oriks back on after the ceremony so they could travel outside. It was considerate, especially for her. They left her room. Soft snores sounded through each room they passed.

The marketplace was empty, the wind whistled through the hides. Kunchok motioned to the side of Dek's structure towards the dark ice. Odesha shivered, rubbing her arm with a free hand. If Dek had said it was safe to go, she would trust him. She had saved his daughter after all. Odesha's feet occasionally tripped over a hidden branch buried deep in the snow. Kunchok moved in front of her, holding both his arms out to her to pick her up in his arms. She hesitated, being this close might be a problem, but she wasn't going to pass up the opportunity. She was going to take the chance to be close to him while she could. Smiling, Odesha held out her arms. Kunchok reached behind her shoulder and knees to pull her close to his chest. They quickened their pace and Kunchok pushed through the snow with his thick legs. Odesha sighed, nuzzling his neck happily. The show of affection caused Kunchok to pause and stare down at her with narrowed eyes. She smiled sheepishly, and he gave a small smile back. They turned a sharp corner around a hillside. The hill blocked her from seeing further, but when she saw where he brought her, she was speechless.

The entire sky was lit up with lights of varying colors. Beautiful hues of pink, green, and purple sparkled along waves of light pulsing through the sky. Kunchok placed her feet back on the ground while she stared in wonder at the magical scene. He pointed a claw towards two rocks overlooking the edge of the cliff dusted free of snow. The rocks had either been sat on frequently or he had prepared them before he came to get her. It was perfect. They sat on the rocks side by side without trying to talk, enjoying the way the colors flowed over their heads. It was like Odesha could reach out and feel their soft touch. She looked up to see Kunchok's reaction, but he just watched her with a soft smile.

Odesha sighed, leaning her head against his shoulder, enjoying this stolen moment with him even if it couldn't last. They sat there for a long time, until her eyes blinked with sleep that she knew she needed. Kunchok stirred, gently moving her head away, to stand up and stretch. He held his arms out and took her up into them again to take Odesha back to her room.

Odesha must have fallen asleep on the way. When he placed her on her bed, she barely stirred. He leaned down and whispered his vow, "Vo lo cos suti ba suta."

Kunchok felt whole again, like a missing piece had found its way back to him. The reactions from Odesha's eyes when she viewed the sky had made him satisfied that he had shared it with her. He had brought her out to see the lights that flowed after Ranna with the full moon high in the sky, hoping she would enjoy them like he did. He was right. The wonder shined bright in her eyes, her lips parted, watching them move. He had never brought another person there, so Dek's surprised reaction to his request to come wasn't unusual. Dek had cautioned Kunchok about the dangers of the ice with a small female, but Kunchok had taken precautions. He had smeared the oil of the orik's feathers across him to keep the predators away. Something had made him want to go there, some feeling deep inside, and he wanted to figure out what that was. The tiny female had made the confusing feelings swirl inside him since he had first met her. He knew what she was to him, but did she know?

A deep, gnawing hunger awakened Odesha. Her eyes flew open when she heard her belly grumble.

Her body felt sluggish. A sudden stab of pain reminded her she had used the ice yesterday to kill the cow beast. When she was younger the pain didn't bother her. She would play with the ice and her siblings in the courtyard at Merdi. Being free to have fun, to play with the magic was what she missed. Then the pain started slowly sapping her joy, the ice building up if she used magic. She withdrew into herself, blocking everyone out without thought.

Odesha thought of the night before. The lights she had watched with Kunchok and his kindness were something she would never forget. The musky smell of the orik was still on her tunic from Kunchok holding her. She jumped up to remove her shift, her hunger needing abated before she did anything, and scooped up snow left over in the bowl to clean herself. After pulling on a light blue gown with large beads sewn on the front, she moved the hanging hide in her doorway to the side to leave, when something on the ground caught her eye. A large piece of cooked meat sat on a clay plate in front of her room. She picked it up, looking around, but couldn't see anyone in the large hall. Who would bring her this? Boni? Kunchok? She snorted. Definitely not Sashi.

Odesha decided to knock on Fanni's hide. A loud yawn echoed from Fanni's mouth when she pushed her own hide to the side, this time, at least, fully dressed, her large tunic covering her from nape to knees. Motioning to the meat, Odesha inclined her head. Shrugging her shoulders, Fanni looked at the plate. The yeti scratched at her head, her furry face frowning in concentration. Fanni was not awake enough to understand what Odesha wanted her to do with the piece of meat.

Fanni mimed eating and instructed, "Yemi."

So not from Fanni. Odesha decided to go along with the meat charade, not knowing how this tribe would react if she gulped down a large cup of blood in front of them.

Oh, the horror.

It really shouldn't matter if she drank blood, but it was hard to argue a point when she couldn't explain it. Smiling, Odesha pointed to her room. She pretended to want to enjoy her breakfast in private. Fanni nodded, yawning louder, and returned to bed with a wave. Odesha listened in the hall to make sure Fanni was asleep again. She walked to Dede's room, sliding the meat under the hide. She didn't smell any taint or poison on the meat. It should be safe for Dede to consume. She would need to go to the shed for blood. A desperate feeling took over as the hunger pains became overwhelming. She'd never bitten another being, it felt revolting to even consider it. Unless it was him.

Odesha shook those thoughts away quickly, not wanting temptation to catch hold. Her feet would take her to Kunchok of their own accord. How embarrassing would that be? Odesha shuddered. Great goddess, she couldn't imagine. She left the keep quietly, the marketplace outside bustling with activity. Her head swiveled, trying to take all the new sights in. The stalls, easier to see in the dim light, were crafted out of snow trees and thick wood. Goods of all types were set out again. No payment was exchanged that she could see. The tribe must all work to help each other. Yeti visited each other, enjoying each other's company. Some tribe members worked at their craft, absorbed in their task. She passed several tanners, a seamstress, and several large forges. The forge owner pounded iron weapons and armor with a giant hammer. The busy place was easy to get lost in, the taller yeti easy to hide behind and to sneak around. They didn't look down much.

Act like you belong, and you will, she thought. Straightening her back, she continued to her goal. The meat shed was easy to spot. It stood deserted on the outskirts of the market. A coppery smell flowed from it, overwhelming her senses. Belly growing with hunger, she checked the area to see if she was being followed. Her heart pounded loudly, the fear of being caught pulsed through her, but she couldn't detect any movement in or outside. Odesha ran inside and shut the door. Her panting breaths were loud in the quiet room. Her belly growled again, her feet taking her towards the back room. The meat from the cow beast she had killed hung in strips from the ceiling, drying throughout the night.

Under each strip were buckets used to catch and dispose of dripping blood. She sniffed the air deeply but couldn't detect any disease or sickness in the blood. The bleeding eyes of the cow beast had worried her, but maybe they were all born like that. The beast had seemed sightless, bearing down on the group of screaming children, moving on pure instinct. The meat could be considered a contribution to the tribe. But she had her own tribe to return to. People that depended on her. It looked like cow beast blood this morning, maybe it was vintage. She laughed at the joke and wished Vashti were there to laugh with her. Vashti would be proud of her for laughing again. Even if it was just with herself. In a yeti's meat shed.

Odesha hefted the large bucket up to her mouth, struggling under its weight. The pains and aches she felt melted away when she took gulp after gulp. She laughed in delight, thankful the old blood went down easily. She lowered the empty bucket to the ground, when a large boom at the door made her whirl around in panic. Her heart felt like it was about to explode. The door slammed closed, the shed shaking as dust rained down, coating her. Odesha reached out for the wall, trying not to fall over.

Kunchok stood at the entrance, arms folded casually. His golden hair was bunched together, small bones were feathered throughout the locks, pronouncing him a leader to the tribe. His sharp eyes never left hers, his size dwarfing the doorway. The giant walked towards her, his loud steps pounded in the quiet of the room. Odesha was so overwhelmed by him she forgot to hold her breath.

When he reached her, it was too late.

Odesha's panting breaths easily brought in Kunchok's clean scent, free of the orik musk. The need for him coursed through her. Her knees buckled, almost sending her to the wooden floor. Eyes wild, unable to concentrate on her thoughts, Odesha tried to get control over the situation with no success. Kunchok stood before her with his dominant presence surrounding her. Odesha tried to hold her breath, hoping she could gather her thoughts.

She kept repeating to herself, is this how she fell to temptation? In a bloody meat shed?

Odesha's nipples peaked and a small trail of wetness began to moisten her thighs. His eyes glanced down her body, nostrils flared, and she knew…he could smell her just as she did him.

The yeti's face turned predatory, his pointed ears stood further on end, and she felt like the tables were turned. It was a new day and the sweet yeti from last night was gone. She was being hunted. And she was pretty sure she craved it, until his arms caged her in.

Then, she was sure.

CHAPTER 9

Odesha's body was locked, trembling. Kunchok's body pushed her harder against the wall. Once her back was against it, she braced herself to take a deep breath, the lack of adequate breathing burning her lungs. His thick scent hit her, and she moaned aloud. She slapped her hand across her mouth, her shock making her eyes widen in alarm. He reached up with his clawed hand and took her hand away. His other hand he used to wipe the blood trickling down the side of her mouth. He held the blood up to study.

Odesha gasped, "Hellfire." Kunchok's aqua eyes flicked back to hers. He didn't understand her words, but he could understand she was worried. He turned to look at the animal strips and motioned to them, miming eating, his intense eyes not missing anything.

Was she still hungry after he had left the food for her this morning?

Not sure how to convey her abnormal feeding habits, she shook her head and placed her hand on her belly miming throwing up. It seemed the best way to show him, even though she thought it made her look ridiculous. She blushed hotly.

Pointing to the thick blood she hummed in enjoyment, rubbing her belly. She looked down in embarrassment, hoping he didn't think less of her. Or toss her out in the snow to fend for herself. What did he think of her now? The need to bite, to mark returned, distracting her from the unspoken question. They continued to stand close together, her nose twitching. Why did he have to remove the musk today of all days? The feeling was unbearable at this point. Small shivers raced through her body, her pale face flushed. Unable to control her body, her gray eyes started to glisten silver, nails extending to hold her prey down.

Kunchok whipped around, walking to the other room, giving her a chance to take a deep breath. He brought back a clay cup held in his furred hands. He bent down to a bucket, scooping up blood with the cup to bring to Odesha. Blushing hotly, she absently felt it was an erotic moment to share blood with him watching, even if there was no biting. For him to know her secret.

Her embarrassment increased when he continued to stare at her, studying her reaction. His eyes narrowed, making her shiver in response. The tension in the room became unbearable to the point she finally caved in under the pressure. She brought the cup to her mouth to sip at the blood, moaning at the salty taste. She swiped her tongue out to lick a small drop of blood on the corner for her mouth, causing him to growl, fangs bared. Odesha couldn't bring herself to fear him. She felt safe with him. His ferocity made her want him more.

Freyja have mercy on them both. If he wanted the good, he would have to know the bad. Kunchok grunted harshly and slammed his arms on either side of her, the cup she held dropping to the floor. It shattered in tiny pieces but neither moved to collect them. His head tilted to the side, watching her reaction to his advance, and moved forward to nuzzle her neck. The soft texture of his white fur made her moan in pleasure, his sharp teeth gliding over her neck to taste. She had nuzzled him last night, but it hadn't felt like this.

His bestial voice growled, "Vo lo cos suti ba suta, Odesha."

And all her restraint was gone.

Odesha's clawed hands rose up, grasping his hair, pulling back with all her strength. His head barely moved, but when his eyes met hers, they sharpened, nose flaring. She flashed her long fangs in aggression, her diamond-like eyes flashing in challenge. He bared his teeth in answer. She lunged forward, their lips connecting before he had a chance to move away. His astonished gaze slid closed. And that's when the fire scorched inside of her. The heat burned a different kind of pain than the ice had delivered in the past. It was consuming. She slid her lips over his, feeling his hard textures. She parted her lips to slide her tongue against his. And he growled deeply, taking control of her.

She moaned in response to his aggression, legs wrapping around him to hold tight. Her arms locked tightly around him. Their tongues dueled together, fighting for dominance, until she pulled away, breathless. His possessive eyes locked onto hers. Licking his lips, he savored her taste. It was her first kiss. It felt so natural with him, her instincts taking over when she tried to dominate him, but he overcame her, taking over the battle. Odesha released her grip from around Kunchok's neck, dropping down to her feet to run outside, catching him by surprise. A roar of anger reached her, making her run faster.

Oh, Freyja what had she done?! Her first kiss. To someone she didn't even know, that could be her downfall. Her death.

Odesha ran until only endless snow was around her, the new blood making her strong. She reached up, feeling ice forming on her cheek, drawing away frozen tears.

The emotions tearing through her were confusing. The fire had started, she had given in to it already, she could feel it. The pain coursing through her wasn't because of the ice, it was because she was far from him. What would happen when she went home? She wouldn't survive if this continued. Happiness, embarrassment, and the unstoppable fire all raged inside her heart. Knowing she had a duty to go back home, but never wanting to leave his arms scared her. He was a leader to the hunters. A position he had worked hard for. How could she ask him to abandon his people for her?

We must always put others over ourselves, Mother had warned. Something Mother never did.

Mother paced in their room, agitated. Her black gown trailed behind her while she muttered to herself. Vashti and Odesha sat silently as they waited to begin their lessons. Suddenly she turned to them, her eyes silver in rage. She gritted out, "Let me tell you a story. Once upon a time there was a princess. She wanted more in life than salt and sorrow, so she made a deal with the devil. "Take me away," the princess said. "But you are not my fire," the devil said. "No, I am frozen. Your frozen queen. Together we will end the war." But the devil warned her, "You may find the fire to melt your heart one day." But the arrogant princess scoffed, "I need no fire. I have ice." The devil held out his hand. The princess took his hand and they made the deal. "

Mother ripped her crown from her head, making the two girls gasp. She held it softly, watching the sapphires twinkle. She whispered softly, "Freeze your heart. Freeze your feelings. Don't let the fire melt you, my girls." Queen Bera threw the crown across the room, leaving the two girls forever alone.

The cold stole Odesha's breath at the memory, her frozen tears falling freely to the snow. Falling to her knees, pressing her face to the snow, she took deep breaths to pull the cold air inside.

Freeze your heart… Freeze your feelings… Don't let the fire melt… It will end you both…

But the fire had already begun. And it would rage until it was satisfied.

Against the snow, Odesha heard the crunch of footsteps approaching. Pushing herself up, she looked up in confusion, drying her face quickly…and noticed a human walking towards her through the endless snow. Odesha blinked her eyes repeatedly, trying to make the mirage disappear, but she was unsuccessful. She attempted to rub her eyes, wondering if she was hallucinating. Well she had done it. The cold had frozen her mind. It had finally happened, great goddess. Laughing hysterically, Odesha grabbed her side, watching the large plumed pirate with shocking orange, curly hair and big black boots continue to stomp towards her. The giant feather was blue, waving about as if it had a mind of its own.

The pirate stopped with hands on the pommel of her sword, leaned forward, and said with a muddied accent, "Alo! Sake pase?"

Stopping her maniacal laughing, Odesha pointed up towards the feathered lady. She asked, "How… how am I? You…you are from the Bijou!?" She had never visited Bijou, but many people on the outskirts of the forest came to court in Merdi to visit. Her father had said from his travels it reminded him of a giant swamp filled with a variety of deadly creatures. He passed through several times on the way from Merdi to Romule during the Blood War to negotiate the treaty with Bera.

"Oui! Oui! Mo du Bijou!"

The pirate's beautiful, warm face was hard to look away from, the cunning sharp in her eyes. "My name is Odesha from Antiqua. What are you doing here?" In the middle of nowhere, she added silently.

The stranger flipped her giant mane behind her. "Oooo smol, la nenaine here to help you parle vit Yeti."

Odesha looked at her in exasperation and pointed out, "I am not a child, madam." She added, "You are going to help me speak the language of the tribe?"

"Oui! Oui!"

Odesha froze with a sudden epiphany. She yelled, "You are a swamp witch!" She remembered stories of the elusive swamp witches that lived in the Bijou forest. There were few left. The witch could bring her home. She could trick her. And she would never see Kunchok again.

The pirate's green eyes glinted with amusement as though she could read Odesha's racing thoughts. "Oui sorceire. Esmerelda." She smiled, showing white teeth.

"Esmerelda, what would I have to give you for this boon?" Odesha might as well go along with this dream sorceress. She had heard of stranger things.

"Une chance parle en." Esmerelda smiled larger.

"You want to speak with someone and if I let you, you will help me learn the language of the tribe?" Odesha repeated in confusion.

"Oui, Kunchok." She nodded her head determinedly.

"Kunchok?" Odesha asked, sure that she had mistranslated. A hallucination wouldn't know of Kunchok, right? How did the witch know? She must have been watching her…

Esmerelda's mouth turned up in a slow smile, the accent gone. In perfect vampire tongue, she clarified, "Your hunter. Wouldn't you give anything for this chance with him?"

The words swirled in Odesha's head like a tornado, repeating over and over. Did she wish this? Mother had warned Odesha away from these feelings, ensuring she remained in this icy shell. Was she willing to bet her life to be with him? The witch was a trickster, Odesha reminded herself. The pirate changed as much as her accent. It couldn't hurt to let Esmeralda speak to someone of her choice in the future, right? For Odesha to take this chance? To stay a little longer?

To finally be…free?

Anything for this chance to be with him, Odesha decided. Odesha's mind made up, she replied, "Oui, Esmerelda. I agree to your boon."

Esmerelda smiled and clapped her black gloved hands together. It made the chains around her neck jiggle. She pulled out a small vial of blood from underneath her red shirt to hold it up for Odesha to see. "Bon appetite!"

Poison? Odesha hesitated, feeling apprehensive. Esmerelda frowned and pointed at her nonexistent timepiece like she had somewhere else to be. Odesha sighed. She reached forward to grasp the glass vial swirling with the liquid. It called to her.

If it was poison, at least it would be quick…

Odesha held up the vial in a cheer to Esmerelda and gulped it fast. It burnt its way down her throat, dispersing through her body.

She vaguely heard Esmerelda sigh, "Time is running out, ma petite. Make them see."

Gasping, the new knowledge Esmerelda had gifted her flowed down her throat, finding a spot to settle deep in her belly, causing her head to spin with dizziness. Falling to the ground, time passed slowly, the world tilting while her mind reoriented. When she looked up, vision settling, the strange pirate witch Esmerelda…was gone.

Groaning, Odesha tried to stand, her belly heaving as her mind felt like it had been split open. The dull light was painful, the softly falling snow excruciating to her sensitive ears. Words pounded through her head, the knowledge she needed so close she could taste it.

She tried to get her bearings. Kunchok was

probably worried thinking a cow beast had attacked her. Odesha tried to form sentences with the yeti's language, but the fresh knowledge was still untouchable, the words disjointedly bouncing around inside her head. When she tried, it came out as a dull croak instead of the grunting tongue. She would have to hear his words to translate them. An idea formed in her mind. She would wait until she spent more time with the tribe before speaking and learn more about them.

The dizziness finally receded, her strength returning. She began a slow jaunt to the tribe. She needed to get back before they missed her or thought her dead. Kunchok had been livid when she had left, she hadn't even told him where she was going. Confident she wouldn't tumble head over heels, she took off in a sprint. The cool air rushed over her and calmed her racing heart. This new chance with Kunchok was exciting. It made her smile with her whole heart. The kiss they had shared was so earth shattering she couldn't wait to experience it again.

Her mind returned to the past.

Vashti and Odesha watched Father on his gilded throne. His impressive might swallowed the already large chair. The largest demon she had yet to see. Alone in this room, she knew his words to be serious, his face lined with stress. "I have grave news, my daughters." Vashti reached over, grasping her hand. He sighed, his head falling to his waiting hand to rub circles into his flesh. His always frazzled hair looked to need a good combing, but that could wait.

"Your mother passed during the night." Vashti and Odesha stood frozen with shock, unable to speak. The king raised his head, focusing on their faces. He hesitated. "Your mother and I were close. But she wasn't my fire. The other half of her soul. She knew this. We spoke of this." He seemed to be lost in his thoughts. He added after some time, "But we had two beautiful daughters even knowing this. She had a drive to end the Blood War. And in doing so…she found her fire. And her fire betrayed her. The fire was something she couldn't withstand without him and she fell to her death."

The pain of losing their mother was unbearable. They vowed to each other to never find the fire, even it meant their own deaths.

The memory had a sobering effect on Odesha's mood. She must be cautious still. The vow didn't concern her, Vashti could be reasoned with and they were only children when they had made the promise, but she didn't know Kunchok's feelings about being together yet. Maybe she could make him understand now that she knew his tongue.

The hunters ran through the market, gathering supplies. Her pale coloring helped her to blend with the snow to remain unseen. Kunchok held his giant weapon standing in the center of the group. He bellowed orders, "Look king bird land! Search! Find Odesha!"

She was finally able to understand him! Wait. What did he say? He was sending a search party to search for her? A funny feeling started in her chest. He cared about her.

His grunts came across as words filtered through her brain. The primitive words were easy to decipher. Odesha rolled the words on her tongue, wanting to speak, but stopped herself, remembering this was a perfect time to gather information. Be cautious. She owed that much to her vow to Vashti. She jogged towards him to stop the frantic search he was amassing with the hunters gathered.

One hunter turned, spotting Odesha. He shouted, pointing towards her, effectively pulling Kunchok's attention to her. His nostrils flared out when he spotted her, firmly shoving through the group of hunters, sheathing his sword, his long legs shaking the very snow in his haste. The group of yeti watched their reunion curiously, waiting to see what the lead hunter would do when he reached her. Odesha stopped running, folding her hands in front of her, remorseful at the worry she caused him. Kunchok clenched his hands at his sides, stopping in front of her, eyes softening.

He grunted for the others not to hear, "Odesha run Kunchok?" Watching her reaction closely, his head tilted in thought, worried he had scared her in the meat shed, losing her forever when he had just found her.

Odesha tilted her own head, loving his gruff voice, and opened her mouth to reply, forgetting her plan for a moment. Instead she coughed, choking out, "Kunchok?"

Their eyes clashed, gray and aqua. He ordered gruffly, "Odesha no run." His dark claws rose, while he ran them down her face gently. The slide of the sharp nails made her shiver in response. "Ice no safe."

Kunchok walked off, calling for his hunters to follow him. The group moved through the marketplace towards the orik forest. Each hunter carried a small pack under their large feathered capes. A short trip to hunt for food in the forest was what the group hoped for. The large tribe required a lot of sustenance, but the dwindling food source made the hunts longer. She wanted to yell out for him to be safe and wish him luck, but the words stuck in her throat. She needed information before she could speak.

Hearing laughter, Odesha turned to see Sashi and her friend from before staring after the hunters. Odesha hurried away from their view, hoping Sashi hadn't spotted her yet through the marching hunters.

Sashi liked to talk. She would be the perfect yeti to gain the information Odesha wanted. Walking off in the crowd of the marketplace, Odesha kept Sashi in the corner of her eye. When Sashi turned away from the departing group to focus on her companion, Odesha ran inside the stall they occupied to crouch in a tight corner concealed by hanging fabric. Sashi's companion stared morosely at the departing hunters' backs, a look of yearning clearly etched on her face.

"Fanni say hunter go?" the companion asked. Both yeti were young, richly dressed in their tunics. Sashi stood shorter, slimmer than the other yeti, holding her shoulders back with confidence. Her companion had a pretty face with soft fur framing it, her demeanor shy.

"King bird land. No meat. No Ranna," Sashi replied carelessly.

Ranna? Could this be their bonding ceremony she watched? Odesha strained to hear more about the ceremony. She eased out from the hanging fabric to hear better.

The larger girl sighed, clearly relieved. "No Ranna?"

Odesha pulled the fabric aside, wanting to see the yeti's face. Why did she sound so happy about Ranna being delayed? This yeti was confusing to Odesha. Sashi was easy to understand. She didn't think of other tribe members' feelings and caused problems wherever she went. Sashi's friend clutched a pink fabric to herself, staring at the piece longingly, swishing it from side to side as if dancing. Sashi maintained her uncaring mood, throwing fabrics around, dirtying them on the snowy floor. They fell to the ground in a mess. Sashi never moved to pick them up.

Sashi whipped her head around and yelled, "Halana no Ranna Boni! Loud hunter. Father hate! Scare king bird. Boni no gift fabric Halana."

Halana's furry face melted at Sashi's words. Odesha's gut twisted. Halana had feelings for Boni, the curious male Odesha had met at the ceremony that tried to speak with her. It explained why she had been so sad they had been leaving, but why would she not want to Ranna with Boni? Because he didn't have enough gifts for her? Or was it only Halana's father that stood in the way?

Halana tried changing the subject. She asked, "Sashi Ranna hunter?"

Sashi jerked her head back dramatically, angry face flashing as she barked, "Sashi Ranna Kunchok!

Kunchok chief hunter. Father approve. Kunchok change. Hairless creature cause."

Sashi twirled around, showcasing a dark red fabric mischievously to Halana. She nodded decisively. "Ranna next."

Halana's eyes widened. "Sashi brave."

Sashi pressed her face close to Halana. She grunted, "Best Ranna."

"Hunters no find meat Sashi? Dek say meat gone. Hard feed tribe," Halana whispered, worriedly twisting her hands. She looked afraid to be questioning Sashi. Odesha understood her fear. Sashi looked to be waiting to explode at any minute with her anger.

Sashi snarled, "Father say Dek lie! Tribe eat meat."

Halana dropped her head, bowing away from the smaller yeti, silent. Halana wasn't confrontational. Her short hair brushed the side of her face, hiding her expression from Odesha's prying eyes. She longed to defend Halana from Sashi. She needed a champion.

The two girls continued to browse the cloth in the stall, lost in their own thoughts. Odesha took the chance to leave, sneaking out the doorway. When swallowed by the crowded marketplace, Odesha disappeared unnoticed. If Sashi tried to bond with

Kunchok and he accepted, she would lose him. Could she choose him over her people? Over her family? Would the head hunter choose her over Sashi and the tribe? Or would it ensure her death...

So many questions raced through her mind. She returned to her room in the chief's keep. She didn't notice Fanni motioning for her from the large open room she passed designed as Dek's throne room. Instead, Odesha entered her own room, pushing the hide closed.

A sharp knocking on the wood surrounding her door startled Odesha. Fanni poked her head around the hide grinning at her. Odesha mimed the sleeping gesture. Fanni's eyes softened in understanding, leaving her to undress and ponder what the future held in silence. She wouldn't worry about Kunchok; that would be unfair to him. The hunters were cloaked in darkness, helping them stay safe from the orik. He was obviously skilled to hold such a high position in this tribe. They would be back soon, she thought before she lay down to sleep.

Days passed as mundane tasks churned in the tribe. She visited the marketplace and watched Dek conduct tribe matters in his throne room. He was fair, like her father, but without the joviality. He was burdened by the food storage and by squabbles within the tribe. It hung heavily over his head. What he needed was a council to help delegate, but Odesha wasn't about to voice that yet. She would when it was the right time. One morning, Odesha wakened with a fresh chalice of blood on her table, signaling Kunchok's return. She drank the spicy blood and pulled a new gown on with excitement. The marketplace was crowded that morning as fresh food and wares were set out to browse. The early morning air felt refreshing, the cold breeze wafting through the tribe, stirring the snow in the air. It had stormed last night, a flurry of snow and ice, and many yeti were cleaning it from their stalls. Fanni stood at the side of a stall helping a merchant remove stone. She waved Odesha forward and gestured to the clearing. Several people were cleaning and setting up sticks that people had dragged. Odesha froze when she realized what they are preparing.

Ranna. The hunters must have found a large supply of meat. They were preparing for another ceremony. Oh goddess, there wasn't much time. Sashi would attempt Ranna with Kunchok at the next full moon.

Odesha dragged an increasingly alarmed Fanni off to the side, floundering on what to do next. Clenching her hands together, she worriedly checked to see if anyone had followed them to their hiding spot. Odesha placed her finger against Fanni's mouth when she was about to protest Odesha dragging her about.

"Teach me Ranna," Odesha blurted out.

Fanni's mouth dropped open in shock, while her hand grabbed at her heart.

Odesha reached forward in alarm, hoping Fanni wasn't having the shock of her life. "Fanni, keep calm, I beg you. My name is Princess Odesha of Antiqua. I live far beyond the orik forest. Err…I mean… You call king bird land?" Trying to flap her arms to get her point across, Odesha hadn't tried to practice the language in her room, this was her very first time speaking it aloud. The words were rusty in her mouth. Occasionally, her own language leaked through to give the sentence more structure. The yeti's way of speech was hard to bring to a basic level and Odesha was so frazzled she couldn't concentrate.

Fanni nodded, speechless.

"I need your help. I'm…I'm falling for Kunchok," Odesha whispered brokenly.

"Fall?!" Fanni looked Odesha up and down to check for bruising from her fall.

"No. No, not fall! Um… Ranna. I would like to Ranna with Kunchok," Odesha clarified.

This language was blunt. Fanni's eyes watered. The happy tears spilled over to her cheeks. Her furry hair stood on end, conveying her excitement. Kunchok was like a son to her since his parents had died so long ago.

"I have to go home, but I don't want to lose him. So that's why I must tell you things. So many things that will change everything. I'm asking you for a private meeting with the chief. Will you help, Fanni?" Odesha threaded her fingers together to clasp her hands to plead with Fanni. She had no one else to turn to.

Fanni's sniffled. She replied, "Fanni ask Dek meet Odesha. Ranna change. Fanni and Dek Ranna many moons back."

Just as the dance styles at court changed, the dance of Ranna changed here as well! She didn't consider that. What she needed was someone who had learned the new dances.

"I'll find someone to help us," Odesha promised. She knew who she was going to ask, but she didn't think that person was going to be happy about it.

"Start when?" Fanni asked, her excitement making her jump in the air. Her smile was contagious, blue eyes sparkling. Odesha knew why Dek had picked this lady to be at his side. She brought happiness out wherever she went, helping Dek's stress to lessen.

Odesha laughed at the yeti's exuberance, thinking for a moment while she relaxed. She replied, "Let's start tomorrow morning. I need a lot of practice in a short amount of time."

Fanni rushed off to speak with Dek, thinking of everything she could teach Odesha. She didn't know if Kunchok would Ranna with a hairless princess, but it wouldn't be for lack of trying.

CHAPTER 10

Kunchok had heard Odesha had been well while he was gone but wanted to see for himself. He watched her walk towards the wooden keep by herself and knew this was the perfect time to get her alone to see how she felt. Did she like being with the tribe? Was their way of life too hard for her?

He worried Odesha wouldn't stay in the tribe if she knew how desperate they were for food. The king birds flew for days looking for meat for their young. They were close to starvation. The tribe was close to starvation.

The beasts of the ice they had hunted in the past had been diminishing. The sickly looking one that had attacked at last Ranna was the first he had seen in a whole year's time. The ice was not a forgiving place for anyone. That was why he didn't want Odesha to run to the ice when he had just met her. He was curious about her and the pull she had on him, and he didn't want to lose the feelings that came over him when she was near. He was starting to fall for the tiny female, he worried. Would she choose him over the other males at Ranna? He bared his teeth. There would be no other male for her. Only him. He would break every tradition to have her.

Odesha walked towards the wooden keep at a sedate pace. Lost in her thoughts, she didn't notice the danger. A heavily muscled arm clamped around her waist. Odesha took a deep breath to scream, but a hand slapped over her mouth, cutting off her air. The tight squeeze made it impossible to fight back as the person pulled her deep into the ice she had been hiding with Fanni in. She panicked, flailing, pulling magic around her to use against her captor when the yeti released Odesha abruptly. He changed their position, lifting her into his arms.

Taking a deep breath, the scent of the yeti flowed through her, making him easy to identify. Kunchok must've been close when she spoke with Fanni, but not close enough to hear her speak or she would have scented him earlier. Her secret was safe for a while longer. She smiled shyly at the large hunter, wrapping her arms around his neck.

"Odesha run?" he growled softly. A bushy eyebrow quirked in question, his hard eyes staring down to her intimidatingly.

Odesha shrugged her shoulders, pretending like she couldn't understand, her smile turning mischievous. She instead chose an easy word taught early to her. "Bulvo?"

Kunchok narrowed his eyes at her playfulness. He growled, "King bird bring meat. Meat hard find. Ranna soon."

Odesha tried acting confused to gain more information, secretly wanting to see if Kunchok had an interest in Sashi. She asked, "Kunchok Ranna?"

He let out a giant gust of air, closing his eyes to nuzzle her neck, the bones of his necklace clacking against each other. She shivered, tickled by his soft hair. He answered, "Ranna. Yes. Vo lo cos suti ba suta."

The last sentence whispered through her mind, jumping around like someone prevented her from understanding. That someone was Esmerelda, she was sure of it. Why wouldn't she let her understand this yet? What was his secret? He said he would Ranna next moon, but with who?

Odesha tensed in his arms. She whispered in her language, "I know you are my fire, forever, even in death. And I wish this was an easier choice for the both of us. I'm not sure what to do." Kunchok's aqua eyes flared with heat when she recited her vow, the emotions flaring between them. He couldn't understand her, but he was still moved by her fervently spoken words.

Kunchok murmured, "Kunchok ask Boni Odesha's name last Ranna. Order Boni bring Odesha meat." Kunchok brushed a small tear escaping Odesha's face with his black claw. "No, Odesha. No cry. Keep safe."

His fur-lined face was different, but beautiful, Odesha realized. The golden hair with swirls of white were carved in the grooves of his face, while his prominent nose, long ears, and sharp teeth proclaimed him to be different. But she was also different to him, yet he still held her tightly. Always protecting her. Odesha's eyes watered after listening to Kunchok's confession. His gentleness, his passion, his love for his people, his attributes—so many things to fall for, to hold tight to. Even if there was a risk. She leaned forward, brushing her mouth against his, trying to convey her emotion through a small kiss. She had no idea what she was doing but had seen many courtiers in forbidden liaisons cavorting about the halls of Merdi. Their lips glided over each other learning the foreign textures. Odesha licked the seam of his lips, causing him to slightly open his soft mouth. Their tongues clashed together as their passion built and they learned what pleased each other.

An unsure virgin and a yeti could be a powerful mix. Kunchok pulled back, his aqua eyes half-mast. He studied her lips questioningly.

He licked his own lips and asked, "Odesha?"

Odesha touched her lips, bringing them to his own. She answered, "Kiss."

"Kisss," he whispered back. A strange word for something that made his heart beat so fast.

Kunchok growled angrily, shocking Odesha. He slammed his head into the ice, splintering the formation. "Odesha no Ranna." He worried Odesha would choose someone else or initiate Ranna without knowing the tradition. He would be unable to warn her. To stop her. She could be with someone not of her true choosing. He wanted Odesha for himself. She was small and beautiful, her white hair like a beacon to him. When he had finally seen her form running from him in the forest after scenting her, he had felt the hunt flare to life inside him. Felt the urge to conquer.

Trying to distract Kunchok from his angry

thoughts, Odesha slipped from his arms, landing on her feet to search for the secret latches to his armored plates. She found two on each side, unclasping them. She didn't know if she would have the chance to do this again. Kunchok felt his armor slipping from his body while Odesha's small hands fluttered over him. He growled, "Odesha no. Ranna. Ranna." He tugged the armor back up, trying to take control.

The yeti must wait for Ranna before they join. That was fine since she hadn't decided what path to take in this journey with him, but they could still get to know each other. She grabbed his hands, placing them on her face. She smoothed her hands down his furry chest. The scars crossing his body told a story of his past hunts and the hard life he had led. The loose dress she wore fell to the side, exposing one shoulder to his gaze. Kunchok zeroed in on the pale skin, his pupils constricting in focus.

Odesha cuddled closer to him, leaning forward to nip at his lips. Kunchok's rigid stance melted with a groan when he captured her lips. His tongue plunged in her mouth, caressing her. The tension built between them as their hands slid over each other, learning their subtle differences. The thick metal of his armor hitting the ground surprised Kunchok. He reared back in shock, staring heatedly at Odesha. The crudely made pants were only held up by a braided belt, making it easy for Odesha to pull at the knot and push them off of him.

Kunchok's cock pointed, thick and distended at Odesha in warning at their continued touches. This was the first part of him she had found to be completely hairless, the appendage standing as long as her forearm. She swallowed in apprehension, unable to tear her gaze away. A low growling from deep inside Kunchok made her shiver. An answering moan whispered through her in response. The heat flared between them, the fire spreading to her belly. A curl of need fluttered deep inside, moving lower as she clenched her thighs together. His hands clenched, fur standing on end when he took a deep breath, scenting her. The sharp teeth bit down tightly, trying to hold on to his control.

"Odesha," he growled with a warning. He needed to lose control, Odesha decided. She wanted the confident yeti from the meat shed. Odesha took a deep breath and reasoned she needed to be the aggressor until he figured out what she wanted. Kunchok's reservations about Ranna were clear, but he didn't understand her. Traditions be damned to hellfire. They may only have today together.

Trysts in the hallway had been a favorite of hers to watch. She remembered the tricks the courtesans used. Leaning forward, she gently licked the tip of his cock, causing him to let out a shout. A loud crack of the ice startled her. She worried the ice was about to fall around them, but Kunchok's claws buried deep sent a secret thrill through her instead. She was doing this to him, making him lose all control he forgot his surroundings.

He growled menacingly. His wild eyes were lost even when Odesha returned to what she was doing. Placing her small mouth to the tip, she slid halfway to the base, moving her hand where she couldn't reach while squeezing gently. She was going to enjoy this. Sliding her mouth quicker to the rhythm of her hand, she quickly learned from his groan how to hold him, how much pressure to use.

Kunchok was babbling to himself, alternating between groaning and growling. He couldn't fathom the pleasure she was willingly giving him, without the promise of Ranna. He had never experienced something such as this, never had an interest before. Odesha brought out so many emotions within him. She used speed to give him his release, pushing her head back and forth quickly. She heard Kunchok release a roar above her, the ice shattering around his hands. It fell to the snow-covered ice, tinkling like bells around them. His thick, hot cum poured down her throat. She struggled to take it all, Kunchok oblivious in his ecstasy. He shoved away from the ice, small blood spots falling to the snow. She scurried to her feet to not fall over.

Some of the ice must've cut him, she mused. He lifted her in the air off her feet. He took them both to the ground, Odesha safely cushioned in his muscled arms. The smell of his blood surrounded her. It consumed her, but she wouldn't take from him now. Honoring his tradition, she would also wait for Ranna.

He grunted deeply, "Kunchok taste Odesha?"

A brief nod was all the permission he needed. Her tunic was pulled over her head, thrown across the snow. She remained breathless, mouth puffy and red. The hunter's eyes darkened with lust when he viewed her furless body, her pale pink nipples tight in the cold snow. Completely bare, she raised her hand to tweak her nipples, eliciting a moan, showing him what she wanted. That set him in motion. Kunchok snarled, battling the savagery he felt roaring inside, pushing her hands away to run his claws down her breasts, making her shiver, slowly circling them, learning them. He wanted to know every part of her, have his touch burned into her mind so she would never forget. The small pink tips tightened, thrusting to the sky. He grabbed her legs, wrapping them around his waist. Locking his eyes on hers, he leaned forward, slowly sucking a nipple in to his mouth, making her writhe in the cold snow.

Odesha screamed, her body bucking, his free hand holding her down. His mouth left her nipples, his tongue licking a long cool path down her stomach. Rearing back, he watched Odesha's reaction, smiling in satisfaction at her mussed state. The pad of his finger traced down her nether lips, parting, feeling. He reared back in astonishment when he raised his hand, wet. His eyes flared with heat as he licked the sweet-smelling liquid from his fingers. Odesha shuddered at the look on his face, knowing he had been pushed to the edge of his fragile control. He leaned forward, slowly circling her entrance when he accidentally bumped her clit.

And her world was lit on fire. Her hips bucked as she screamed. Her reaction astonished him. He circled the small nub gently until Odesha babbled incoherently. He left her clit behind, moving lower. Whining, in agony, looking up at him accusingly, Kunchok smiled back.

His confidence grew at her response to him. Kunchok circled her opening, finger gingerly dipping inside. Leaning backwards, he seemed to be worried about something. He pushed on her walls and remarked, "Odesha tight." He prodded her entrance, learning what she liked.

Odesha reached up, sinking her claws into his ass, needing release. The fire was scorching inside her, unable to be quenched without it. He bellowed out, sliding his finger in again, slowly pushing in a second.

He seethed with clenched teeth, "Odesha bad." She fell back, releasing him from her claws as she twisted her hips, moaning. He increased the pressure until she screamed her release. The fire calmed, her frantic need sated for the moment. He gently removed his fingers, licking them when he left her hot center. He wanted to stay here in their icy cove with her. Away from the constant worries and needs of the tribe he sought to meet. She wrapped her arms and legs around him, holding him close as her breath returned to normal. Kunchok nuzzled her neck. Odesha sighed while squeezing him tight, wanting the moment to last forever.

Dek's voice echoed across the snow. He yelled Odesha's name, interrupting their quiet thoughts.

Hellfire, she forgot about that meeting. Kunchok stood up, looking at her curiously, wondering why Dek would call for her at this time. She shrugged her shoulders and tried to look for her gown he had ripped from her. She would tell him of her meeting with Dek after Ranna, she promised herself. She would tell him everything.

"Odesha go?"

She pointed in the direction of the voice. She answered, "Dek."

Kunchok nodded his head. He fastened his plates and pants back, then leaned down to nuzzle her neck one last time. He stood tall, looking at her seriously as his pointy ears folded back to his head.

"Kunchok return. Two moon time. Gather hunters." Sadness engulfed her at the news, but at least she'd have time to practice Ranna. She knew the tribe came first. He wouldn't let them starve and he wanted the hunters to participate in Ranna if they so wished. Odesha placed her hand over his massive chest, praying silently she could win the heart of this great hunter. That she was enough.

Odesha's name flew through the air again, more urgent this time. She pushed away from Kunchok, his small grunt making her turn and wave sheepishly. She tried to follow Dek's booming voice while making herself presentable. The ripped gown and her head full of snow must look dreadful.

Dek stood at a stall in the marketplace, waiting for Odesha to arrive. He turned when she called his name, waving to get his attention. He drew back when she was close enough for him to get a good look at her appearance, his face shocked, his hair standing on end.

Odesha stopped walking towards him. She blushed fiercely in embarrassment. They drew a strange sort of attention from the marketplace. She must look worse than she thought.

Dek shook himself from his stupor and approached Odesha, grabbing her arm to pull her towards the wooden keep. He tried to stay in the shadows away from the crowd. Which was impossible giving his size and status.

"Chief Dek, I must…" Odesha tried to explain. Huffing from being carried around, she wanted to give some sort of excuse to her appearance.

"Quiet Odesha, tribe listen," Dek grunted softly.

Fanni must've explained her secret to Dek. That was convenient, she didn't want to explain from the beginning. Odesha sent a silent thanks to her friend for helping her. Finally making it to the keep, Dek pulled the main hide closed. He took Odesha to his room. She stumbled inside when he let go of her arm. Fanni sat at their table. They were going to use the chief's private room for this meeting. When she noticed Odesha, Fanni gasped and clutched her chest in fright.

Fanni screamed, "Great beast attack Odesha?!" Odesha ran to the ice mirror in the corner. Her dress was on backwards and her hair looked like a wet bird nest littered with ice, snow, and a couple branches.

Odesha gasped, trying to pull a few branches away, but it didn't help.

"Fanni! No, I was…" Odesha paused, trying to think of what to say. This was awkward, but the truth was always the best. "I was with Kunchok." She clenched her hands, worrying about what they might think. Ranna was sacred to them. Dek's laughter boomed out in the larger room. Fanni swatted him on the arm to quiet him. He continued to laugh, bending over to hold his belly.

Fanni turned a darker color, hair standing on end. She reminded Odesha, "Tribe wait! Ranna!"

Odesha sighed, attempting to be vague, "We just kissed."

Fanni looked confused, "What kiss?"

Odesha forgot that they only nuzzle. "Touched lips together. Courting in my country."

Fanni still looked confused, squinting at Dek's lips hesitantly as though they might jump from his face and come for hers. She didn't look impressed.

Dek cleared his throat, shaking his head at Fanni. He asked, "Odesha speak Dek?" Dek kept his eye on Fanni while she practiced "kissing."

Odesha shook her head at Fanni for distracting her from the important meeting she had wanted. Fanni didn't notice. Her lips were awkwardly puffing out and in at Dek.

Clearing her throat, Odesha explained, "Chief Dek, I would like to Ranna with Kunchok next moon. I am from Antiqua. A large tribe across king bird land. Antiqua has a big castle, many people, and many markets. But Kunchok can't leave tribe. He must bring food to tribe."

Odesha worried her lip, hoping she hadn't overstepped her bounds with Dek and Kunchok. Dek sat back in his giant chair, watching Odesha in thought. His large bones decorated his frame proclaiming him as the chief, the chosen tribe member to make decisions. Fanni, giving up her practice of kissing, alternated between sitting and standing from the bed with worry, distracting Odesha.

"Who chief Odesha's tribe?" Dek finally asked.

Odesha braced herself, not knowing how the tribe would accept a female leader. She replied honestly, "I am the chief. My father is the chief of the tribe I came from." Maybe if she threw her father in it would be more acceptable, but she was proud to be the leader of Antiqua. She hadn't had much time to practice, but while she was there, she had made several improvements.

Dek looked astonished. He asked, "Woman chief? Much food in tribe?"

"Yes, I am a woman chief. Big chief gave me the land.

There is much food, many choices." She took a breath, getting ready for the big confession. "I am a vampire." Odesha continued, "Vampire. I am a blood drinker. I can't be in the sun or heat for a long period of time."

Fanni gasped at her confession as if she was the one standing in a heat dungeon. Being this far north, there wasn't much sun at all, but the sky was still beautiful.

Odesha hurried to say, "I do not drink tribe blood. I prefer animal blood. I cannot eat meat. I become sickly." The simple language was a nuisance! She struggled to explain before the couple became more alarmed, casting her out to her death. Dek nodded his head, worry clearing from his face as he reached an understanding of what she was. He motioned Odesha to continue. So, she did. She told him of her family, Antiqua, the salt mines, and how she arrived. They sat together for hours, learning their history, disturbed only by Dede occasionally poking her head in and Fanni tending to her.

At the end of their long discussion, the room was silent. The chief absorbed all the new knowledge Odesha provided. His head bowed in thought, Dek grunted, "Much Dek think. Odesha want Kunchok?" A sense of the past permeated his mind when he had heard the word "vampire". A story passed down from his sire's father long ago, but it was elusive to him.

He looked up to see Odesha nod in the affirmative. Dek tilted his head curiously, "Kunchok want Odesha?" Odesha hesitated, nodding in the affirmative again. He might not have said so, but she could feel it in her heart. Even if she had to poke Sashi's eyes with icicles. Freyja forgive her, she sounded as bloodthirsty as Vashti. Kunchok had protected her from the orik and had warned her away from the ice. He came to find her when he returned from his hunt and thought of her needs right away. The blood she could have gone to get for herself, but he knew she felt uncomfortable sneaking around, instead delivering it to her.

Dek smiled. "Fanni. Help Odesha learn Ranna."

Fanni squealed on the bed, arms thrown wide in joy as she scrambled to her feet to join Odesha.

Dek's smile disappeared as he turned, asking seriously, "Odesha's tribe accept Dek's?"

Odesha reeled, astonished, trying to picture the tribe in Antiqua. Something she hadn't thought Dek would ever consider. She recalled the vast differences of people already there. They were accepting of all species already. "Yes, there's much land for Dek's tribe."

Dek nodded his head. He had much to think about, but neither choice was going to be easy.

"Decide after Ranna. Dek think." He clapped his hands, rose from his chair, and left the room, calling for Dede. Odesha couldn't be happier with the results of the meeting. She had gotten everything she wanted and more.

Fanni whispered, "Dek worry tribe. Sleep Odesha. Hunters gather. Practice Ranna tomorrow."

CHAPTER 11

Odesha hid in the large clothing stall in the marketplace, hoping to catch her prey. She had found its weakness. She had already watched its movements. She heard the quiet thud of soft-soled feet coming towards her, the soft grunt of a question from the front of the stall, and knew it was time to spring her trap.

A soft, distressed gasp reached her. She leapt out, brandishing her weapon fiercely when her prey turned to her in astonishment.

"I need your help, Halana!" declared Odesha brazenly, hoping they hadn't attracted too much attention yet from the other stalls in the marketplace. The soft blue cloth Halana lovingly gazed at every day sat securely in Odesha's arms. The perfect bait to lure her in.

Halana's eyes widened. She pointed towards Odesha and shouted, "Furless creature speak?!"

With a sigh, Odesha muttered, "Yes, furless creature speaks." She cleared her throat, motioning to herself, holding tight to the fabric. She clarified, "I'm happy to meet you. My name is Odesha."

Over the last couple of days her grasp of the language had greatly improved. Fanni had explained to Odesha she was under Dek's protection, so she had access to anything in the marketplace. That was when her plan formed.

Odesha gestured back to the cloth, "This soft blue cloth, it's perfect, yes? Perfect for Ranna with someone special."

Halana whimpered in distress, the pain in her eyes intensifying.

Odesha gently moved closer to the skittish yeti. She didn't want to frighten her away. She whispered, "I would like to give it to you."

Halana's body stiffened as her head shot up, looking questioningly into her eyes. Odesha nodded firmly, hoping Halana saw her sincerity. She repeated, "Yes, I will give this to you if you promise to help me."

Halana's face turned suspicious. "Why furless creature need help?"

Her face turned a soft pink, Odesha replied

slowly, putting emphasize on her name, "Odesha would like to learn how to dance for Ranna."

Halana, stunned at the request, looked from the cloth to Odesha, making her decision. "Sashi won't like." The sides of Halana's lips twitched with a repressed smile. Sashi didn't like much, but this would send her into a rage unlike anything the tribe had ever seen.

Odesha agreed seriously, "No, Sashi definitely won't like. Could you help me learn by next Ranna?"

Halana reached out, running her hairy fingers down the soft cloth lovingly. It was what she had dreamed she would wear during Ranna to Boni. But that was a forgotten dream. Maybe just having the cloth would be enough. She whispered, "Yes. Halana help Odesha Ranna next."

Odesha smiled, triumphant. She handed over the soft cloth to its new owner happily. She had captured her prey.

Let the lessons begin.

In the dead of night, Odesha left the wooden keep, hurrying to the secret meeting spot with Fanni at her side. Of course, with all the giggling Fanni was doing, they probably didn't go unheard.

"Fanni. You must stop giggling so loudly. You are waking the whole tribe!" Odesha attempted to whisper-shout to her friend who found this hilarious, almost doubled over with her laughter.

Fanni tried to stifle her laughter. She said, "Fanni sorry. Laugh late night."

Odesha snorted, unladylike. "Or it could be all the loma you had at dinner."

Fanni smacked her lips. "Tribe make yummy loma Ranna. Fanni taste. Tribe hate rotten."

Odesha groaned. She muttered to herself, "I can't believe I'm dragging a drunk yeti around in the dark for dance lessons! How far I've fallen, Freyja." Odesha looked up the heavens in complaint when Fanni's giggles continued. Odesha shook her head, moving quicker, finally having spotted her intended destination in the hidden area in the ice formation.

"Who Odesha get help?" whispered Fanni loudly, stumbling in the entrance. She kicked at a large tree branch hidden in the snow. Pointing her finger in at it, Fanni began to lecture it as Odesha watched in astonishment.

Goddess help them all, she was talking to the vegetation now. Halana popped her head out of the ice formation, trying to see what the commotion was. Fanni took a deep breath to yell out to Halana in greeting, but Odesha made it to her in time, slapping her hand over the yeti's mouth.

"Fanni, remember, we talked about secrecy. Halana is going to help us," whispered Odesha urgently.

Fanni nodded, eyes wide. Odesha took Fanni inside as best she could, deposited her on an ice cap with a huff. Fanni struggled to stay upright, finally propping herself up with the branch she had just berated.

"Thank you again for coming to help. Both of you. This means the world to me," Odesha said, dusting the snow off her hands. She was already exhausted and hadn't danced a step yet. Halana nodded, her furry face drawn in concentration as she sat on the ice cap next to Fanni.

Curiously, Halana asked, "Odesha dance before?" Odesha nodded, stretching out in the snow with light breaths.

Halana narrowed her eyes suspiciously, "Show Odesha dance." Halana's lips quirked while she watched Odesha's continued stretches, chasing the sadness from her eyes. The furless creature was amusing to watch. Odesha hummed to herself, thinking of different dances she had been taught at court, picking the fluid line dance. It was a lively jaunt she enjoyed dancing in the past.

"Alright, I'm ready," Odesha said to her audience. She shuffled far away from the two, hoping there was enough room. The dance started off, arms wide as she hopped from one side to the other, legs kicking outward, the dance performed so many times at court it came naturally with no thought. She followed the steps finishing with a flourish and a hand clap, turning to find her captive audience looking at each other.

Fanni and Halana started to laugh uproariously.

Odesha tried to shush them. Feeling hurt, she put her hands on her hips to march over to her audience. She asked, "What part of 'quiet' did you two miss?! What's so funny?"

Halana hiccupped as she tried to control her laughter. "Odesha no Ranna like baby king bird hatching shell. Ranna tribe. Ranna shousha."

Confused, Odesha turned to Fanni to translate, never hearing of this word until now. "Shousha?"

Fanni pointed to her chest thumping herself emphatically and said, "Shousha."

Soul, whispered through Odesha's mind.

"Each tribe Ranna different. Shousha guide tribe." Fanni hummed to herself, slapping her large hands on her hide dress making a thump, thump, thump, sound like a drum. She nodded to Halana. Halana bowed her head in shyness, standing slowly.

Her body swayed softly, arms moving to the beat. The dance displayed her soft soul. Her large frame hid an inner grace. Odesha felt the sweetness of Halana's spirit, her kindness. Her body movement helped the mood in the small enclosure turn relaxing and calm. She stopped, hair standing on end when she realized she held a captive audience. She hurried to sit back down on her ice cap, ears moving back and forth in distress, rubbing her arms.

"Halana, that was beautiful. Thank you for showing me your shousha. Any member of the tribe would be lucky to have you," Odesha said softly, gently touching her arm.

Fanni nodded her head. She agreed, "Halana big help tribe. Chief say Halana best cloth worker."

Halana's hair stood on end even further, showing her embarrassment. She murmured a small, "Thank you." She tried to turn the attention away from herself, looking up to Odesha. "Deep inside shousha stay. Feel?" Halana closed her eyes, placing her hands over her chest. Odesha sat down on an ice cap adjacent to them, closing her eyes to feel her spirit, trying to get a grasp on what she really felt.

The fire. The ice. Battling for ground inside her. The fire raged inside of her, hungry for release, like a volcano ready to erupt. The ice stood nearby waiting to consume her. To make her fall in a comfortable sleep forever encased in its grasp.

"Yes. Yes, I feel it," whispered Odesha.

"Release shousha," Fanni ordered. She hiccupped loudly, almost falling over.

Odesha groaned, opening her eyes, "I can't though."

Halana tilted her large head. She confusedly asked, "Why?"

"Mother always told me to control the fire," Odesha murmured absently to herself. "And what if I do decide to release myself in front of the tribe? I'm afraid I will scare them. The vampire inside me wants out." Odesha groaned again as all the reasons she shouldn't dance filled her head. Her head fell to her hands, knowing she couldn't show her true self to these gentle people. She was so afraid that they would turn from her, when she had finally found the place she belonged, beside Kunchok.

Odesha felt a furry hand grab her free hand and looked up to see Halana kneeling in front of her. She softly said, "Parents no always right. Tribe shousha change. Bad. Good. Ranna sacred tribe. Ranna love."

Odesha looked into Halana's eyes thoughtfully. Her suggestion was helpful, but Halana couldn't recognize what held her back from Ranna. Odesha whispered so Fanni couldn't overhear, "Maybe Halana should listen to Halana's own words."

Halana's eyes widened at Odesha's statement. Her hand trembled slightly. Odesha knew Halana secretly wanted Boni, but she was afraid.

Fanni interrupted, hiccupping, "Odesha drink blood. Tribe no care. Odesha save tribe last Ranna." She snorted with a thought, "Halana remember Otari Ranna? Otari kick Rulf hard. Bed many moon. Rulf no hunt." Fanni and Halana reminisced together on disastrous Rannas in the past, their easy-going ways giving Odesha hope.

Odesha stood up from her ice cap, startling the two yeti, fists clenched with determination. "I hope you two are right because you may be my only friends left after this Ranna." Odesha raised her fist in the air. She could do this. "Let's try again."

Fanni shushed her, giggling, finally serious. Halana clapped softly in encouragement. And Odesha let loose the fire.

CHAPTER 12

Odesha practiced every night with her friends. Occasionally she saw Kunchok with the hunters, the fierce looks he sent her way keeping her hope alive. She watched him with his people from a distance. He organized his hunters to lead them to their last hunt. She realized most of the burden fell on his shoulders, Dek more of a decision maker. The wise leader that kept the marketplace together. Kunchok kept them alive and fed. Together they were a team.

Kunchok was gentle with the tribe's children, bringing them trinkets from his trips. The hunters, he ruled with a firm hand. Her admiration for him grew with each passing day.

Odesha walked through the marketplace, getting fresh air during the middle of the day. The tribe was having hunter training with the younger yeti in the clearing they usually reserved for Ranna. Kunchok led the training with wooden swords and stuffed orik on posts. Dede walked towards the group, dragging a wooden sword twice the size of her, huffing and puffing with her effort. Kunchok noticed her, leaning down to speak quietly in her ear. She nodded sheepishly, handing him her sword, standing by his side. He noticed Odesha standing there gawking at the two of them and smiled softly.

He stood, calling to the group, "Dede help teach today. Soon first girl hunter." The group cheered, holding their swords up in celebration. Dede blushed prettily, holding her chin up proudly. Kunchok had included her in the training, promising her a spot in the hunt even though Dede was a small girl. It was surprising that the tribe was already thinking progressively when Merdi was stuck in the olden days where women couldn't fight.

Kunchok tasked the hunters with going on the last hunt before Ranna to gather more meat. From the whispers, Odesha figured out the tribe had thought what they gathered previously would last, but they were wrong. The people were hungry, and rationing was starting to cause unrest. She could see the worry on Fanni's face when Dek came back at night. Odesha could hear the talk in the marketplace growing among the people, but something else had been weighing heavily on her mind.

The fierce pirate lady in the snow.

Where did Esmerelda come from and why would she help her? What did she have to gain besides a simple promise? The last comment Esmerelda had made didn't sit right with her either. Make them see, she had said. Make the tribe see what?

Her mind full of thoughts, Odesha absentmindedly walked towards the group Kunchok was training in the circle. The hunters gathered there with their packs of provisions, shopping the stalls a final time while Kunchok was busy training. Odesha had a fierce urge to see if Esmerelda was still out in the snow. If she could answer her questions.

Suddenly it felt vital. A clawing need, making her wander away from the tribe. Odesha's heart beat faster the farther she walked. She walked for what seemed like forever until the orik forest disappeared. The sparkling white landscape was calming and quiet, until she spotted a shocking blue feather standing on top of an orange mass of hair. Esmeralda lounged on an ice cap, gazing into a barren snowy field alone. She looked lonely sitting there. Odesha called out, alerting the pirate to her presence.

Esmerelda turned with a smile, reaching a hand out to help Odesha up the jagged ice she sat on.

Esmerelda exclaimed, "Bonjour, ma petite!" Her pixie nose looked small in her heart shaped face, brown eyes sparking with mischief. She was older than Odesha. Laugh lines were etched around her eyes and forehead.

Odesha huffed, "Bonjour, Esmerelda. Do you live out here in the snow by yourself? It seems lonely." Dusting off the snow, Odesha settled beside the peculiar woman.

The pirate laughed, holding her giant scabbard tightly, replying, "Non." Face sobering as her accent changed, she added, "I haven't had a home in a long, long time."

Odesha felt sorry for the eccentric witch sitting there with no one. She pushed her white hair out of her face to ask, "Could you answer some of my questions?"

Esmerelda smiled sadly, "Oui. You want to know so much. But I think these are the wrong questions. You see, we are almost out of time, no? A storm is coming, they hope to consume us. To bring back the past we worked so hard on. Even now they test their boundaries." Esmerelda sighed, looking into the distance. She whispered forlornly, "I can't see them anymore."

Odesha leaned in to ask more questions, trying to figure what in hellfire the witch was going on about, when Esmerelda placed a finger to her lips, hushing her. The witch's calm demeanor shifted. Looking around her wildly, she pulled her sword from her side, the inscriptions carved in the shining blade glinting in the snow. Esmerelda's focus narrowed in the darkening distance. She grasped the sword tightly in front of her, pushing Odesha behind her. The skies continued to darken, a rotten smell permeating the freezing air. Odesha shivered, but it wasn't from the cold. It was from the aura of menace pulsing towards them, like a sickness spreading across the land with the threatening clouds.

Esmerelda shouted, "Get down!"

Odesha crouched on the ice out of Esmerelda's path, trying to see the source of the gut-wrenching smell in the darkness while the storm clouds continued to build. Silent lightning was beginning to streak across the clouds, giving the appearance of a spider moving its legs.

Odesha squinted when she noticed a movement through the lightning. Pinpoint red dots shone brightly close together. Eyes. The two dots were eyes. The heavy breathing of the creature was piercing across the distance. Odesha shivered. She could see the outline of the shape now, the hanks of wet hair hanging, the bloody trails falling from its sightless eyes.

A true monster from the deep. It was as large as a lion, moving quickly towards them. Spittle flew from its fanged mouth. She had thought the cow beast was diseased. It had been only the beginning. This being was truly death running towards her. The skin hanging down looked to be rotting.

Esmerelda released a battle cry, swinging her sword in the air. Odesha tried to be brave in the face of this beast but let out a small whimper. Its eyes seemed to see into her very soul, locking her in place. Before she could blink, a large bone spear cut through the distance, sticking in the creature's leg, pinning it to the shattered ice. It screeched in anger, turning on the object holding it from its path. It snarled at the offending spear, ripping it from its leg with its teeth. The bone spear splintered, giving way. As soon as the spear was free, the monster stopped its motions, its face suddenly slack.

The eyes dimmed as if lost.

Like a puppet on a string, the head fell to the side, its body dropping to the ground to slide back across the ice into the lightning. The darkness engulfed the beast, swallowing it whole. The clouds parted and scattered to all sides of the sky after the monster's disappearance. Shards of low light filtered through the menacing clouds, breaking them down until nothing remained.

Esmerelda faced the direction the creature had come from, looking from side to side, checking to make sure the danger had passed. She relaxed her stance.

Brown eyes blazing, Esmerelda asked, "We are almost out of time. Will they die? Or will you convince them to live?"

Odesha heard the shout of her name, stopping her reply to Esmerelda. Kunchok's long, lumbering strides tore through the snow. Odesha relaxed with his presence. He made her feel safe when he was near. She turned back before she forgot her reply to Esmerelda, but the pirate was gone, along with the storm. The odd pirate was truly frustrating, disappearing when Odesha needed real answers.

Kunchok reached Odesha, grasping her arms to check for wounds. He had seen the creature advancing on Odesha on the ice cap. He had thought he was too late, throwing the bone spear at the last minute. He asked desperately, "Creature bite Odesha? Odesha hurt?!"

Odesha shook her head frantically, trying to convey she was unhurt. Kunchok looked angry. His hair was standing on end in agitation and his eyes moved all around them to check for danger.

∽

"Where Odesha go? Why Odesha gone?" His shouting escalated as he asked his questions. She was supposed to stay at Dek's home for protection, didn't she realize that? He had tried to tell her the dangers of the ice before.

Kunchok growled deeply, "Every night Odesha leave Dek's hut." He gritted his teeth from saying more. Kunchok had heard reports from the guards he had posted throughout the tribe hiding in the snow that Odesha left with Fanni every night. Several other tribe members had been disappearing at night as well, but she was the one he had been concerned about. What they did was unknown since the guards were ordered not to leave their posts. But he was going to find out after this Ranna, he had promised himself.

He was jealous! Odesha thought delightedly, before she found herself upside down suddenly, over his shoulder, his large hand holding her bottom. His strides took him to the bone spear buried in the snow. He picked up the least damaged piece in case he needed to defend them from another beast before he made it back to Dek's home. Odesha tried to pull her tunic down to cover her important parts exposed to the winter weather, wiggling on his shoulder in distress at the tribe seeing them like this, but she didn't blame him. Leaving unprotected without telling anyone where she was going again wasn't the best decision.

"Odesha want other tribe? Vo lo cos suti ba suta." The last sentence he growled hard, menacingly.

Odesha frowned in concentration at the phrase again, but she was unable to translate it.

Hellfire to sorceress tricks! Esmerelda had blocked it from her mind! Kunchok walked through the marketplace. Some tribe members stopped to watch the spectacle, shaking their heads with their disbelief.

She huffed as Kunchok spoke again, "Kunchok hunt Ranna. Back two moons. Odesha stay Dek home."

Kunchok deposited her on her bed. While she sprawled out, bouncing on the feathered area, he left hastily, still angry over her near miss with the crazed creature. Her death would've mattered to him. Couldn't she see the tribe accepted her as one of their own?

Halana, Fanni and Dede visited her in her room,

asking what had happened when Kunchok left. Tribe gossip spread quickly through the marketplace.

Odesha described the creature that had attacked her, and Kunchok's intervention, leaving the part about Esmerelda out, not ready to share her quite yet until she knew Esmerelda's intentions.

"Kunchok save Odesha!" squealed Fanni, holding her heart at the romantic notion.

Odesha sighed, "Yes, Kunchok saved me. I'm exiled to this room until he gets back." She frowned in mock sadness. "Halana, I'm sorry, you'll have to bring our Ranna dresses in tonight so I can help you sew."

Halana's ignored her request as she asked, "What Odesha tribe wear?" Her brown eyes blinked innocently.

Odesha thought about how to answer Halana's question, remembering a dress Fanni had brought that had been too large for her. She reached over to her bedside table stacked with neatly folded cloth, pulling out what could be a tent at home, molding it over herself to show a basic example.

"It's fitted at the top, see this, Halana? It cinches your waist to appear more feminine. It flows down to your feet, falling in waves, but the bottom is different compared to the person's shape. The latest style was a large necklace to sparkle with the dress."

"What necklace?" Halana frowned in concentration.

"A necklace usually contains stones hanging, like Dek's bones hang from his neck." She hadn't seen anyone other than Dek and Kunchok wearing them yet, only beads adorning hair.

"Chief wear bone necklace," Halana stated emphatically.

Odesha tried to explain better. She added, "Chief wear bone necklace, yes. Women wear stone necklace." Halana frowned, envisioning that type of necklace in her head.

Odesha reclined on her bed, giving her friends room to sit. She explained, "Frankly, the court dresses are stifling. Oh, they are beautiful, that's for sure. When the women dance with the men at court, it's absolutely magical to see."

She hummed a melody softly to the group, remembering the dances.

Fanni piped in, "Tell more Odesha tribe!"

So Odesha talked more about her home, relaxing with friends she had never imagined having.

CHAPTER 13

Odesha ran up to Fanni's hide, pounding on the wooden door frame. "Fanni! Fanni, it's Ranna day! I must've fallen asleep after you left. Halana didn't come by during the night to finish the sewing!" She was frantic, worried she wouldn't be able to participate and win over Kunchok. She hadn't even bothered to comb her hair or change her tunic, running from her room to wake up Fanni in desperation. Fanni groggily opened the hide, groaning softly. Odesha wondered if she had been taste testing the loma the night before again because her eyes were reddened.

Odesha sighed miserably, "I don't know what to do, Fanni."

Fanni groaned in misery at Odesha's loud words, her head pounding with pain. Scratching her furry arm, she smacked her lips, replying, "Fanni forget. Present Odesha." She walked back in her room, Dek's quiet snores echoing throughout the hall. She came back, dropping a small, fur-wrapped package in Odesha's hands. Running her fingertips over it gently, Odesha decided she wanted to wait until she was alone before she opened it.

Remembering Odesha's initial worries, Fanni replied, "Fanni find Halana. Ask Ranna dress. Men return last moon. Ranna tonight. Get much rest." She suggestively wiggled her large furry brows, causing Odesha to giggle.

Odesha, distracted by the present she held in her hands, said her goodbye, running back to her room holding it tightly to her breast. Sitting on her bed, she unwrapped the fur all the time wondering what it could be. The small rope untangled easily, falling softly to the bed. Inside, diamonds sparkled in the dim light. She lifted it up and gasped, recognizing it. The coronet from Antiqua. The one she was wearing when she was trying to escape the orik. Her eyes watered at the small piece of home, at the memory that felt so long ago. It must've been picked up by a hunter during the chase, somehow in perfect condition. Suddenly determined to find Halana to make sure their Ranna dress was done, Odesha realized was ready for the night to begin.

Running excitedly through the marketplace, Odesha didn't even remember to knock before entering Halana's small home. She pushed the hide aside and announced, "Halana, I'm ready for…holy Freyja, what's wrong!?"

Odesha ran to Halana. She was sprawled over her sewing desk, sobbing uncontrollably. She gently stroked the large yeti's back, waiting for Halana to speak. Halana's sniffles slowed when Odesha helped mop her wet fur with a stray cloth. "Sashi visit," whispered Halana miserably.

Odesha gasped, "What did that witch do?"

Halana bit her lip. She answered, "Sashi talk Ranna Kunchok. Sashi see Halana dress. Sashi angry. Say mean word." Halana's large eyes flow with fresh tears. "Sashi tell Halana Boni no good mate!"

Halana's body shook with her sorrow, the unstoppable tears splashing on the desk. Odesha thought Sashi was the worst type of friend for Halana, preying on her innocence and good nature, but this was cruel even for her. The large yeti was beautiful in her own way, especially on the inside. Halana's family must be important to her to influence her so.

"Halana, Sashi is jealous of you. Can't you see that?"

Halana looked up in astonishment. "Sashi jealous? Odesha drink Fanni loma?"

Odesha snorted at this. She was beginning to doubt if there was any left. "No, I'm serious. Sashi is a bitter, selfish friend. She sees the good inside of you and wants to attack it. To take out your light that shines so bright. Your dress you made for Ranna shows her she can't influence you. She's not able to change you."

Halana replied swiftly, "Sashi rotten. Halana afraid see Sashi Ranna." Odesha giggled, Halana eventually joining in, mopping up her tears with a piece of fabric.

Odesha reached to the table she had placed the hidden package saying, "I have a gift for you Halana."

Halana perked up, looking at the small package holding the small coronet. Halana let out a soft grunt in astonishment. She whispered in awe, "Pretty stones. Small Halana's big head. Odesha keep. Halana wear dress. Halana give Odesha."

Halana hurried to her pile of cloth, rummaging through it. She held up her own wrapped package to Odesha. "Odesha Ranna dress done."

Odesha's eyes widened. "I was so worried it wasn't done! I was going to spend all day helping you sew."

"Halana fast sew cloth. Halana come Fanni's hut. Help Odesha dress Ranna. Eat first."

"Thank you so much, Halana. Bring your dress too. We'll get ready together, there's plenty of room."

Odesha hesitated at the doorway. "Halana? About Boni, he is a good tribe. He has a good heart."

Halana nodded her head shyly, staring at her pile of blue cloth. She had always known that, but she had to find her own confidence first.

The women congregated at the marketplace, empty of men, breaking their fast. They chattered happily about the coming night. Odesha hurried past them, waving her greeting in response when they called her name. She had become friends with many of the tribe members at market and knew most by name. Odesha was going to visit the meat shed before Ranna tonight, needing more than just a chalice of blood. She rushed off to do that.

A high pile of sticks sat in the clearing, ready for the fire to be lit. Several freshly crafted wooden tables sat around the fire. The circle designed for dancing was clearly designated in the dim light. Odesha stared at the circle planning her dance steps and how far she could move. The meat shed door slammed shut. A large male exited, wiping his hands on a cloth while scooping up more snow to clean himself. He walked towards the huts in the distance, oblivious to her presence. She hurried inside, shutting the door to drink from the fresh buckets. When done, she ran back to Dek's home.

It was time to get ready to make the choice that could affect her entire life.

The darkening sky had the tribal yeti at the ceremony already shouting for loma. It was truly the beginning. The nervous flutters of Odesha's heart beat loudly. Fanni waited for Odesha patiently in her room. Fanni was dressed in her Ranna clothing, sitting on the bed, sipping from a large chalice of loma already. The chalice was made so large, Fanni was barely able to wrap her hands around.

Odesha chided her, "Fanni, so help me if I have to drag you around again on this Ranna day I will give tribe blood a taste!" Her smile showed she wasn't serious, but Fanni didn't realize that. Fanni hiccupped in distress, placing it on the bedside table, adjusting her green bandeau top, trying to hold her giant breasts in the scant fabric.

Odesha shook her head. What an interesting night this was going to be. The thump of footsteps reached her. The hide was pushed to the side. Halana stepped through, holding the stack of packages she had been preparing in her room when Odesha had visited.

Odesha hurried to help her, bringing them in to

place on the bed. She asked, "What all do you have here, Halana?"

The yeti handed over her items to each person. She replied, "Halana sew many present. Fanni open present. Odesha open." Halana sat on the bed beside Fanni, grinning happily. The tears were dried from her face and her hair was brushed to a perfect sheen. Fanni gently opened her package, occasionally letting a hiccup escape.

"Halana give Fanni rock?" Fanni asked in confusion.

Halana snorted loudly. "Odesha tell tribe story. Necklace. Halafren make Fanni necklace." Fanni gasped holding up the small stones to see clearer. The amber stones were beautifully carved, threaded with hide string to hold the stones around Fanni's neck.

"Lisha vo Halana. Stone pretty," Fanni whispered, tying it around her neck.

Odesha asked curiously, "Who is Halafren?"

"Brother," stated Halana, with no emotion.

Odesha gasped excitedly, "You have a brother, Halana?! Why haven't I met him yet?" She would have loved to meet a brother of Halana.

Halana thought for a moment before answering, "Halafren loner. Work hands market. No hunter. Father no happy."

"That explains why your father is so set on you

mating with a hunter for Ranna," Odesha remarked casually. Halana nodded, distressed. "Your father still cares for Halafren, doesn't he?" Halana nodded again, hesitantly. "Then wouldn't he still care for you, if you found happiness? I would think that would mean more to a father than anything."

It would mean so much to her own father that she had found happiness after sending her to Antiqua. Odesha opened her package carefully. White threads caught the light of the glowing candle. A criss cross of fabric formed the halter neckline of the small top, small bones woven in. The second piece, short white fringe, fell in the front, growing longer in the back. Halana had deftly woven the fringe around strips of fabric so peeks of Odesha's flesh would be shown, but not too much.

Odesha turned to Halana. She whispered with awe, "This is more than I could have ever imagined. But…bones? I thought only Dek could wear?"

Halana nodded her head sagely. "Leader wear bone. Odesha leader. Show tribe Odesha leader."

"This must have taken much work and time. Thank you. Thank you from the bottom of my heart, Halana." Halana nodded her head sheepishly. Odesha noticed a lone package sitting unopened on the bed, adding, "What's in the last package?"

Halana sighed. "Halana Ranna dress. Halana no

wear." She had changed her mind many times on her way to Dek's home.

"Show us!" commanded Fanni, sneaking a large gulp from her chalice behind Odesha's back. She put the chalice back, turning around with a smile of innocence when Odesha's narrowed eyes cut to her. Halana opened her package slowly, holding the long blue cloth aloft for the two women to admire.

"By Freya's ghost, it's exactly like I described," whispered Odesha. The blue cloth had been crafted into a long court dress, cinched at the waist. The flow of the fabric looked beautiful against Halana's skin. She would look like a princess from a foreign land.

"The whole tribe will be jealous of your beauty, Halana. If you won't wear it, I won't go out there," Odesha promised.

Halana blushed. "Hurry. Change dress. Before Halana change mind."

Odesha laughed as her friends help her dress. The cloth Halana had made her fit perfectly, the gently swish of the fringe inspiring her. She hummed to herself, moving about the room.

Odesha called for the ice magic, weaving the fringe into sparkling icicles. The tinkling sounds caused by the icicles clinking together flowed through the room. She placed the sparkling coronet on her head.

Fanni cleared her throat to explain, "Kunchok chase Odesha king bird land. Protect. Odesha fall. Kunchok find Odesha. Keep stone safe." Fanni pointed to the coronet on Odesha's head, explaining where they had come from. Odesha's eyes softened at Fanni's confession. Kunchok had kept the coronet safe for her, even though it was replaceable. He didn't know that and had kept good care of it for her to have again one day.

Fanni chided, "No melt pretty ice." Fanni reached behind her to a second chalice sitting on the wooden table, handing it to Odesha carefully. Bewildered, Odesha took the cup, looking inside. Blood. Fanni nodded her head to the unspoken question when Odesha looked to her.

Kunchok.

Even though she had drunk the blood from the meat shed earlier, this would help warm her before Ranna. A dessert for the dance about to take place. Fanni brought an ice mirror forward for the women to view themselves.

Halana stood in her long blue gown, a painted blue stone around her neck. The yeti looked soft and feminine, ready for the celebration. Her brown eyes sparkled with a hidden excitement. This was the first Ranna she had ever looked forward to.

Odesha's body sparkled in the moonlight, the icy

bones clicked together, her long white hair flowed to her waist. The icicles concealed her body depending on her movements. She felt like she was truly showing who she was today. A frozen vampire princess.

Fanni bounced on the bed in excitement, her stones nearly smacking her in the face as she tried taking another quick drink from the large chalice. Her eyebrows wiggled over her blue eyes when Odesha quirked her own eyebrow at her. Halana chuckled out loud.

They were ready.

CHAPTER 14

Nearing the edge of the ceremony, the tribe congregated together. Laughter flowed throughout the tribe joined together for this one harmonious moment. The yeti present had imbibed much loma already from of the look of the empty wooden barrel on its side near the benches. Sashi stood beside the second loma barrel alone, drinking deeply.

The clipped red cloth barely concealed her private areas, small strings holding it together. The mated women looked at her with barely concealed disgust at her appearance.

Fanni, Halana and Odesha walked together, shoulder to shoulder. Conversations stopped. The large crowd watched their approach. Their eyes traveled from Halana's long dress to Odesha's fringe style with envy. The tribe whispered at the bones Odesha proudly wore, proclaiming her status. They remarked on the necklaces the women wore, feeling their own barren necks. Odesha kept her head held high watching the crowd silently. They reached the middle when the drums started, low and booming.

The women's chatter increased. They stood tall to fluff their fur. Their attention was turned to a group approaching in the far distance. The excitement raced through the crowd. The group of men had arrived, carrying the large spit of meat to roast.

Kunchok led the silent hunters, helping to carry the front. Their silver plates glinted in the firelight; the long white feathered capes flowed behind them. It was other worldly, but Odesha only had eyes for Kunchok.

His long hair flowed past his shoulders, while small bones tied in the strands declared his title. The pants he wore were tucked into his hide boots that were laced up to his knee. The harsh expression he was wearing would've scared many courtiers from Merdi, but his savagery only excited Odesha.

Kunchok directed the men to place the animal on the spit already prepared for their arrival. They hefted the animal into the air, securing it tightly to the spinning wood. The hunters spread out after finishing their task, the single women bringing loma, stumbling over themselves to serve the men while trying to gain attention.

Odesha and Halana watched silently, admiring their men from across the clearing.

Halana inhaled sharply beside Odesha. Boni held tightly to the end of the spit of the meat, standing proudly. It was an honor to carry the meat. Boni had helped greatly to distract the king bird dropping the meat from its claws into the nest during the last hunt.

"Kunchok no see Odesha," Halana whispered, distracted. Halana knew Boni wouldn't notice her. His eyes never stayed on her for very long at a time. But this time was different. He was chewing on a piece of meat when he spotted her, swallowing roughly. He ended up choking on the meat, bending over at the waist, trying to push it from his throat. A large hand bouncing on Boni's back from Halana's brother, Halafren, helped bring the meat up. Boni nodded with his thanks, rubbing his sore throat, not meeting Halana's eyes again, embarrassed at the spectacle he had just caused. Boni had always thought himself beneath the shy Halana. Halafren was a good friend to him and had never mentioned Halana's interest in him. He had thought Halana's silence meant she was uninterested. She was the most creative and gentle lady he had ever known. Boni would never try to reach for her even though that was what he wanted more than anything.

Sashi delivered a loma and plate to Kunchok, trying to move close to his side to get his attention. She pressed her breasts to Kunchok's arm, trying to make him notice her when Odesha's eyes met Kunchok's own annoyed stare.

Now he sees me," she whispered back to Halana. Kunchok's eyes flared with heat, the bones in his hair trembling as he reared his head back in shock. The plate in his hand shattered with a slight clench of his hand. Sashi's hair flared with distress, withdrawing from his arm. Sashi tried to push the clay shards from her wet fur, while fleeing into the crowd in anger, all the while giving Odesha murderous looks.

Odesha smiled in delight, winking an eye to tease the hunter staring at her. He didn't seem able to move to retrieve another plate. She was trying not to act bothered, but all she wanted to do was jump in his arms and have him carry her away to his hut. But that was not Ranna. And she would follow their tradition this night.

Kunchok's body gave a shudder, as he tried to shake himself from his astonishment.

Dek released a booming yell, high up on his dais. He was early this night. "Ranna begin. Big moon high. Tribe meet after Ranna."

The crowd continued drinking, celebrating their night. The single men stayed distant away from the women, the anticipation increasing as secret stares were stolen across to each other.

Halana looked down at her long blue dress after seeing the envy from the tribe women. She really did feel like the princess that her friend had described. And she finally had a true friend for once, never realizing how Sashi belittled her when she tagged along with her. Odesha raised her confidence, helping her realize she could be with Boni even though he isn't the strongest, quietest, or most effective hunter. Instead he was funny, always making her laugh when she was down. He was talkative when she just wanted to listen, and he was kind to the other hunters struggling. All his qualities were appealing to her. She was going to take Odesha's advice and fight for her man. Well, in this case dance for him. Halana straightened her back in determination, listening to Dek begin Ranna. His booming voice echoed over the tribe that listened to his every word. He stomped his large foot, feathers and fur extending, letting loose a howl to the moon marking the beginning. The tribe formed a circle. The hunters howled back to Dek in response.

Halana's racing mind finally stopped, and she knew what she wanted to do. She chose her happiness over her family's wishes for once.

The drums pounded, quick and loud as the tribe circle widened. Odesha looked up at Halana, wondering if she would take a chance to Ranna Boni. Halana was silent, eyes wide, as she stared at the tribe standing in the circle. Please, great Freyja, give her the strength.

Kunchok left the dais where he had been speaking with Dek, hopping down to stand beside the hunters. Dek wiggled his eyebrows alarmingly at Odesha. Fanni had been teaching him things it seemed. Kunchok stared at her with narrowed eyes, trying to understand why she was standing in the circle. He was going to stand close by in case he needed to intervene. Odesha knew he wished she understood Ranna, he had said so himself. What he didn't know was that she was ready for it. She took a deep breath, readying herself, taking a step forward to the middle of the circle when Halana's outstretched arm stopped her from entering.

Kunchok stepped forward in shock hoping to stop Odesha before she made a choice she would later regret. His eyes burned with menace, thinking she had been about to attempt Ranna and had no idea what she was doing. Afraid that she could choose another male on accident without knowing, he growled deeply, making several of the hunters look at him in apprehension. They stepped sideways to get away from him before he pounced on them.

Pulling her eyes away from Kunchok's increasing agitation that she could do nothing about, Odesha asked, "Halana? What's wrong?"

"Halana first. Halana no change choice." Halana smiled down at her, relieving Odesha's increasing worry. Odesha's mouth dropped open in astonishment when Halana grasped the front of her beautiful gown firmly, raising it to walk in the circle as elegant as a courtier from Merdi. The drum beats lightened in their intensity. Halana glanced around nervously, shyly, as Odesha cheered for her friend. Inside she felt like biting at her nails, but that wouldn't be wise. She would make Halana nervous as well. She would stand proud and happy, showing Halana she had confidence in her choice.

Fanni sat beside Dek's throne, fanning herself nervously with her clay plate. The loma she held in the other hand sloshed to the floor. They hadn't talked about who would go first. Fanni didn't know Halana had decided to dance against her father's wishes and it was causing her to panic.

Halana took tentative steps forward as she adjusted her hold on her gown, swishing her skirts, gliding about the room gracefully to the beat of the drums. She stopped in front of the group of hunters as they postured, showing their muscles. Kunchok kept his eyes fastened to Odesha. Halana pushed them all aside roughly, reaching inside the group to grab Boni, dragging him forward.

Boni's blue eyes were so wide Odesha saw the color from her side of the clearing. His astonishment was evident, his face a dark red at being the center of attention. Halana let go of his arms, stepping back from the center of the circle she had led him to, executing a deep flourish curtsy that Odesha had taught her to show respect to him. Messy hair flopping on his head, Boni was trying to watch Halana's entire dance as she continued to dance carefully around him in her beautiful dress.

The drums stopped.

Halana stepped close to Boni, leaning in to peck him lightly on the lips. She turned slightly to Odesha, winking at her in thanks. Somehow, Boni looked like he could melt to the floor he was so entranced by the beautiful Halana. He stepped forward, hesitantly giving her a small kiss on the lips in response and the crowd erupted with cheers.

The tribe yelled, howled, and carried on for the new couple. Halana and Boni left the center of the ceremony, their fur lifted in excitement. Before they exited the edge of the circle, Halana reached for Boni's hand to stop his retreat to their new hut they would share once they mated. He looked back at her in confusion, but she held up a finger, nodding to Odesha, folding her hands like a sentinel while she waited for her friend to make her move. Odesha had encouraged her to make a choice based on what she truly wanted, and Halana would stand by her as she made her own.

Odesha felt the pressure inside her build as the low beat of the drums started again. Locking eyes with Kunchok standing in the center of his hunters, arms crossed, Odesha tentatively walked forward. Kunchok's eyes widening in panic, holding out his hands to warn her to stay back until they could understand each other, when a bright red streak cut across the circle to the gasps of the crowd.

Sashi made her way towards the clearing, the drums increasing at her hasty entrance. She danced without pause, her lewd movements making Odesha blush, the small scraps of red cloth couldn't hold her in, the top falling to the ground. Her gyrating hips took her to the hunters, reaching out to grab Kunchok. His repulsion was evident, his large arm trying to shake hers loose, but he stopped trying to get free when he realized he could hurt her if he struggled.

Locking eyes with Odesha, he stared hard, trying to send his thoughts across to her, worried she still didn't understand what was happening and wouldn't intervene. He could still say no to Ranna with Sashi without Odesha's intervention, but it would shame Sashi in the tribe. Odesha thought he looked angry at being pulled away from the hunters, his feet dragging, but not wanting to break Ranna tradition.

Odesha winked at him, trying to calm his raging emotions. His face showed his confusion to her gesture. He turned around to face Sashi when they reached the center of the circle, unable to contain his horror at the spectacle she was portraying, moving around him crudely with not an ounce of grace. Looking heavenward, Kunchok couldn't stand to look at her anymore. Some members of the tribe shook their heads in disgust, turning their own backs dismissively.

Odesha noticed Fanni nodding her head up and down furiously towards her, her now broken clay fan flapping uselessly in her hand. The drum beats changed when Odesha pushed her way forward. The tribe became curious at the low murmurs and the exclamations of surprise, many turning back around to see what had happened. Odesha entered the circle, causing Sashi to pause in her gyrations, following Ranna tradition to give her rival a chance to dance. She stood stiffly to the side to give her room, glaring furiously at Odesha. The hate in her eyes was palpable.

Odesha moved gracefully towards Kunchok, her gray eyes firing silver.

Ice and fire raged inside her, battling. Voices whispered through her mind. Freeze you heart, before the fire starts.

Her fangs descended.

This was her hunt. Her hunter. Her spark. Her flame.

Kunchok began to pant as he eyed her fangs.

He knew she was dangerous, felt the urge to flee. But he was as much a predator as she was.

She let loose her power, but for the first time there was no pain. The fire inside her took over when she embraced it, her choice made, for good or bad. The ice melted from her heart, gathered in her hands to shoot up to the sky, never to enter her again. Time moved slowly, the very air moving to her needs. She beckoned the snow to come to her. It fell softly, the tribe gasping when the magical flakes blanketed only inside the circle they had formed. It felt like it was just the two of them, hidden from the crowd in their moment. The icicles on her skirts felt cold against her skin, their tinkling became louder as she twirled to the slow drum beats.

Fueling the fire inside, the drum beats were insistent in her ear, loud and booming, she pulled the snow to her, letting it caress her body, her long limbs twisting and turning to the rhythm. She released her passion, her soul, to the tribe that had saved her, accepted her.

Kunchok, unable to look away, was captivated by her, mesmerized. She stopped gracefully in front of him, a large snow shower shooting up to the sky with a flick of her hands like fireworks, causing the tribe to gasp in awe. The drums ceased beating. The final decision had to be made.

Kunchok didn't hesitate with his decision. He ran to Odesha, determined, arms wide to clasp her to him. He clasped her face tightly, whispering in awe, "Vo lo cos suti ba suta, Odesha."

The words finally translated through her mind, clear for the very first time.

You are mine now and forever. A promise of a love forever that they would share together. He had been saying it since they had first met. He had known they would be together for that long, and she hadn't known.

She stared into his aqua eyes with realization, finally saying the words in his language she had held in all this time. "You are my spark. My fire. My love. Now and forever."

He growled in response, their mouths clashing together with need, the tribe gasping, but they ignored them. She clasped his head, her fingers entwining with his long hair. Dek shouted a faint warning in the distance. Odesha opened her eye to see Sashi advancing on them, a small blade raised high in the air to drive in Kunchok's back. He didn't know, couldn't see her!

Odesha shoved away from Kunchok, twisting around him to grab Sashi's arm, trying to grapple with the larger woman's strength, but the blade was descending towards her faster than she could stop it.

Kunchok let loose a bellow, grabbing Sashi, throwing her away from Odesha before the blade could pierce her heart. The hunters hurried to restrain the crazed yeti. Sashi screamed an unholy sound of rage, her tears tinged with blood.

Where did the blood come from?

Dek jumped from the dais, Fanni fell over in a faint in her chair. He motioned to the hunters. "Hold Sashi. Tribe meet Kunchok. Choice."

Kunchok nodded in acknowledgment, dismissing Sashi from his mind until later. He had a new mate to take care of. His large legs ate up the distance towards Odesha, scooping her up in his large furred arms. Nobody could take her from him. He returned his mouth to Odesha's while he carried her away to his hut, the tribe cheering for their happiness, Sashi's rampage was forgotten for the moment. Dek must've woken Fanni from her faint. She was now standing on the dais shouting in happiness, arms thrust in the air. Dek had a hold of her so she wouldn't fall off, shaking his head with a sheepish smile. Halana smiled with more joy than anyone had seen in the tribe, her laughter contagious. Boni wrapped his arms around her shoulders, leaning down to whisper in her ear.

The snow poured down from the heavens, celebrating the tribe's happiness of their lead hunter finding his mate. Odesha restlessly moved against Kunchok, trying to find relief from her growing need. He turned his head, biting down on her neck in admonishment for tempting him. Instead of calming her, it had an opposite effect, turning her need into a frenzy as she threw her head back and moaned loudly.

He paused, growling softly, "Hold." She barely had time to lock her arms around his neck before he took off running, clearing his doorway in record time. She felt the feathered bed beneath her as he stripped from his plates. She ran her fingers through his soft white fur, feeling the hard muscles underneath. She noticed hairless patches with raised scars painted on his torso of battles hard fought in his past, giving him a dangerous edge.

He ripped the straps from her body, growling at having to wait longer at having his mate. "Beautiful. Mine."

His grunts became more garbled as he kissed down her body, marveling at her softness. He gently licked her cunt, moaning at the flavors exploding in his mouth from her wetness. Odesha screamed when his tongue worshiped her clit, her orgasm exploded, fireworks shooting behind her closed eyes. Body relaxing, the fire burning inside her was now a comfortable slow burn. Kunchok pulled himself up to his elbow and growled, "Open. Watch."

Her eyes flashed open just in time to see him grab his large cock, running it up and down her nether lips in preparation, testing her wetness. He leaned down, kissing her wildly as their tongues twisted together and placed his cock at her entrance, pushing through her tightness. She knew her first time was going to be uncomfortable and twisted away from him with a whimper, but he brought back her pleasure, rubbing her clit with one hand. A dark claw tweaked her nipple. The pressure in her low belly built as another orgasm began. She moved her hips forward, trying to find the perfect spot. He grabbed her hips, thrusting in deeply through her small scream, while trying to tear through her barrier quickly to stop her pain.

"Gone. Pain gone." Kunchok's eyes were glazed with pleasure, her tightness causing him to want to thrust hard, but he didn't want to hurt her again. His hair fell around them, curtaining them in their own world. She smelled his fresh scent free of the orik musk, driving her wild. Rotating her hips, she adjusted to his size, wanting him to move. He held still, letting her.

Finally, she grabbed the sides of his face, pulling him to her. "Please…"

He snarled, thrusting hard, unable to stop. She screamed in pleasure, arms thrown wide on the feathered bed when he grabbed her waist to pull her up to him, his long cock stroking her very core, rotating his hips, shoving her higher as their pleasure became unbearable. The orgasm she had chased pierced through her, hungry for release. She tensed when the urge hit her…

Bite.

The descended fangs waiting to strike ached. Odesha twined her arms around his neck, latching her nails tightly to him, pulling him close.

She whispered in his ear, "Forgive me." The tip of her descended fangs entered the bend of his neck, the sweet blood of her mate rushing through her. Kunchok roared his pleasure, the bite pushing him past oblivion, shoving even harder inside her, crushing them together over and over. She released him, letting out her own scream; his blood dripped from a corner of her mouth. He zeroed in on the trail, leaning in to lick at it, still thrusting inside her hard and shifted positions to lock his mouth around her neck to give her his own bite of acceptance. His mate went wild in his arms, biting him in the chest, fangs sinking down hard. Overwhelmed, Kunchok's pleasure burst through his body with a war cry. He felt the cum rush up when her scream joined his own and let it loose while her wet pussy milked every drop.

Kunchok's hands gave out, falling to his elbow to catch his fall, stopping himself from crushing her. Odesha wrapped her arms around him tightly, licking the last drops of blood on his neck. He pulled back to look down at his mate, stroking her face reverently to ask, "Odesha speak Kunchok?"

Odesha blushed, her secret now out, but exactly how she wanted it. She replied shyly, "Yes, I wanted it to be a surprise for Ranna. I asked Fanni and Halana to help me learn Ranna, that's where I was those nights that I disappeared from Dek's home."

Kunchok chuckled. "Kunchok sorry. Kunchok protect Odesha. Kunchok worry Odesha Ranna other hunter." Suddenly feeling a twinge in his neck, he winced slightly, rubbing it with a smile. "Odesha bite?"

"Yes, it's how we Ranna in my tribe. Well, we have a wedding, but my people bite to become closer to each other." She touched the healing spot gently. "It will bind us."

Kunchok nodded his head adamantly, "Forever. Odesha drink Kunchok. No meat shed." He loved the thought she would bite him to feed, that he could provide this for her. The pleasure he received from it was indescribable. He started to rise from the bed,

Odesha stretching her naked body out to ask, "Where are you going, Kunchok?" She growled softly, teasing him. "Do you think to escape our Ranna night?"

His fangs flashed in a smile, gently kissing her on the top of her head. "Kunchok sorry. Tribe council. Choice. Odesha come."

She pouted, "But what about Ranna?" He smirked, circling her entrance with his finger, "Odesha hurt. Heal. Ranna forever." She winced, maybe that was a good idea.

CHAPTER 15

Heading towards Dek's home where the council was about to meet, Odesha and Kunchok talked about Antiqua. She explained how she learned his language. That confused him. He hadn't seen Esmerelda during the fight with the creature. He had been too worried about Odesha, he explained.

A pirate lady in the middle of the snow with bright orange hair was hard to fathom, she admitted. He was quick to catch on, listening to every word she said even though she added her own language. He would stop her to clarify a word and she would try to explain. If she could get him to learn her language, they would have more complex conversations. She looked forward to that. When she described her family, he asked more questions, trying to learn more about them, smiling at the stories she told of them.

When she asked about his family, he told her of their passing at an early age and Dek helping to raise him. Fanni had already told her the story of his past, but Odesha had wanted to hear it from him. They turned their conversation to the council meeting, but when Odesha asked Kunchok about Sashi, the conversation abruptly ended. He became agitated at the reminder of their near miss. He had tried to block it from his mind so he didn't become angry on their Ranna night. He didn't want Sashi to cloud their memories.

They had come close to losing each other. If Sashi would have killed Kunchok…

Odesha reached up to his hand to clasp it tightly. His eyes moved down to hers. She smiled to reassure him that it would turn out alright. Their love would be what she remembered from their Ranna night and how they had fought for it and won. When they reached the tribal dwelling, Kunchok grabbed the hide, holding it back for her to step through. She thanked him and walked inside, looking at the tribe members that had gathered for the meeting. Kunchok indicated to sit next to Fanni, who waved frantically, smiling like she won a giant case of loma.

Sitting down beside Odesha, Fanni reached over

and patted her furless hand. Odesha smiled slightly to her, shaking her head, but wouldn't say anything in response. On the high throne sat Dek with his silver plates fastened and long feathered cape. Kunchok sat at his side. Dek nodded to Odesha when she caught his eye, then turned to Kunchok to whisper in his ear. Dek stood up, turning everyone's attention with the sound of the bones shaking from his wooden staff. Holding his arm up, he yelled, "Tribe gather. Choice. First choice come."

The hide of a side room was jerked aside. Two male yeti dragged in a screaming Sashi. Spittle dripped from her mouth, coating the ground. Her legs hung uselessly. She was not attempting to flee from the crowd. An inhuman wail left her throat, her bloodshot eyes staring holes through Dek with anger. The two guards dodged her continued assault from her manacled fists and nails until she reached the center. They dropped her, securing her hands to the same type of bonds Odesha had been placed in when she first arrived.

Dek watched her calmly. "Sashi. Daughter Patcha. Ranna sacred. Sashi knife. Kill Kunchok. Sashi want steal life. Choice." Dek sat down in his chair after his speech, listening to the eerie silence in the room. Sashi had tried to kill their chief hunter in the middle of a sacred ceremony. They weren't going to take this decision lightly.

Kunchok stood and shouted for the tribe to hear, "Kunchok first. Sashi kill Odesha. No forgive. Sashi Ramdak." As he sat, many nodded at his quick decision, agreeing with his choice.

Odesha turned to Fanni for a translation. She asked, "Ramdak?" This word wasn't translating correctly, several words bounced around in her head. Banish. Exile. Extradite. Sacrifice.

Fanni whispered back, "Sashi no tribe. Sky take Sashi. Ramdak."

Dek tilted his head. "Tribe choice?" He was waiting for someone else to give him another option, always the fair leader, but the silence was heavy in the cold room, broken only by the snarls from Sashi. This was a proud people with old laws ingrained in them since their youth. They had to honor those traditions and beliefs.

Dek knocked his staff on the ground signaling the end to the decision. "Tribe choice. Sashi Ramdak." A loud sob from one of the elders slashed through the crowd. He covered his face with his clawed hands, another yeti comforting him.

Fanni nodded towards him. "Patcha. Horm hold. Halana father." Horm was consoling Patcha, trying to counsel the elder through his distress at losing his daughter.

Sashi's unfocused eyes stared menacingly at the leaders refusing to reply to her sentence. She never looked to her father. The guards pulled her upright to better hold her. Unholy screams ripped from the young yeti's mouth as she was lifted to her feet. Odesha felt only sadness for the young yeti and her family. Sashi was obviously crazed now. The creatures that came from the sky would kill her quickly. She had seen how dangerous they were. The guards pulled keys from the pack at their side and reached to unlock her bonds to take her outside. She stood docilely, continuing to stare blankly at Kunchok. Hearing the chains hit the ground, her eyes hardened, changing before them. Sashi screamed, twisting her body around to the guard nearest her. She climbed over his body like an animal would. He attempted to throw her off, people beginning to scream hysterically. Sashi reached to grab the sword pommel hidden in the guard's cloak to pull it free. Dek and Kunchok rushed towards her, their own swords pulled free to stop her before she tried to kill the guard. Instead, she had other plans.

Sashi turned to Kunchok, sword held out proudly. She screamed, "Ramdak?! No. The sky will use me no longer."

But the language she used wasn't of the yeti people. It was said in the vampire tongue.

Turning her sword, she drove it into her side grunting. Her eyes widened, bloody tears slipping down her face. Collapsing slowly in the center of the clearing, the dark blood widened around her, staining the floor where she once stood bravely.

The tribe elders fell to their knees. They sobbed as one of their own joined the spirits. The chaos afterwards took a while to calm down. The people generally thought Sashi had been speaking gibberish. But Dek and Fanni had heard the vampire tongue and recognized it. Dek looked to Odesha for clarification, and Odesha nodded her head placing over a finger over her lips. Dek agreed with Odesha, turning away at the unspoken request, not wanting to stir the crowd into a frenzy at what Sashi had spewed in her final moments. He wanted it to be over with. Kunchok and Dek sheathed their swords, turning back to their seats.

Dek cleared his throat, ordering hoarsely, "Sashi first choice join spirit. No Ramdak. Patcha take Sashi." The elderly Patcha's crestfallen face was hard to see. The yeti had lost his only daughter in a manner of moments in front of his own eyes.

The guard retrieved his sword, swinging the fallen yeti's body into his arms, walking out silently with the grieving Patcha. Horm stood at his side, helping his dear friend through the pain. Patcha losing Sashi had made Horm realize he needed to set some things right with his own children. He had been blind too long. The sadness in the room continued, but the sobbing slowed while people returned to their seats to hear Dek's second choice. The tribe was resilient, facing death every day. Tears cleared fast when a member of their group sacrificed themselves instead of facing the consequences they invoked.

"Second choice. Tribe hope grow. Moon past, food hard hunter take. Dek send hunter king bird land. Tribe survive. Kunchok lead. Kunchok hide king bird nest. See Odesha fall. Watch Odesha close. Save Odesha stuck in snow. Dig. Kunchok's two hand bleed. Odesha save Dede. Save tribe. Odesha learn tribe speak. Odesha speak second choice."

Odesha worriedly nodded to Dek. She hadn't expected to speak in front of the tribe elders. She had thought Dek would lead the entire meeting, but she was the best to explain. Clearing her throat softly, she found the words deep inside to speak. This choice affected so many.

Make them see. The words of Esmerelda whispered through her. Odesha cleared her throat lightly, beginning to speak about her land, the mines, and the needs of her people. She reverted to her training, watching the reaction of the yeti. Some expressions were easy to read.

Incredulous. Suspicious. Hopeful.

The end of her speech pulled from her heart, "... my people need help in the mines. And you need help. We could benefit from each other. Please... Please... Come to Antiqua, to my home, and help me make it our home."

Dek stood, arms held up once more, asking the tribe for their decision. "Choice change tribe. Tribe follow Dek Antiqua, Odesha home? Tribe stay?" At the end of their joined speech, the room sat silent while everyone tried to absorb the new knowledge. This was a large choice that would change their entire dynamic. A new land with plentiful food was hard to believe.

A richly dressed yeti stood tall, calling out loudly, "Dek lie tribe food! Patcha say food much."

Kunchok stood with hair flaring out in challenge. He argued, "Yorin no hunt! Kunchok hunt. No meat. Beast gone ice! Soon tribe starve!"

Yorin backed away from Kunchok's challenging stance slightly.

"Where meat?"

"No tribe track. Gone. Sky take. Yorin find?"

Yorin shook his head dejectedly, sitting back

down. That argument was over quickly at least. The large Yorin didn't want to venture across the ice, instead sending Kunchok to do the work for him. One elderly yeti stood to bang his walking stick on the ground. One by one, the elders stand, continuing to thump their sticks on the ground in rhythm. They had made their choice.

Abruptly, Fanni stood, waving her arms boldly in the air making horrific squeals of happiness. The whole room burst with life, people standing and laughing, a welcome change from the sorrow and tension they had just experienced.

Something big had been decided.

Kunchok and Dek smile together. Dek laughed, announcing the decision, "Tribe leave Antiqua, Odesha home! Three moon!"

CHAPTER 16

Kunchok took Odesha's hand, leading her across the snow to the icy field. Odesha smiled up at him in anticipation. The lights were going to be sparkling across the sky tonight and Kunchok had promised earlier they would go to their secret spot. This time they would be able to talk to each other through it. Kunchok decided to swing her up in his arms. He loved to hold her, and his legs made the journey easier for her.

Odesha ran her fingers through his soft hair. She asked, "Why did you bring me here after the first Ranna?"

"Kunchok see Odesha smile sad. Want Odesha happy," he murmured nonchalantly. She was sad watching all the new couples at the last Ranna, he was right, but she didn't know that he had noticed.

"Were you angry after I killed the cow beast?" she asked curiously, remembering the look he had sent her when the beast lay there dead.

"No. Kunchok worry Odesha. Beast no safe," Kunchok replied. The ice cliff came into view, the bright lights flowed overhead, this time in varying colors of blues and grays. It reminded Odesha of Kunchok's eyes with his varying moods. The lights distracted her from the person waiting for them. Esmerelda waited for them, swinging her legs off the cliff staring up at the lights, lost in thought. Kunchok growled, sensing the magic swirling around the pirate. Odesha called out a halting greeting. Kunchok placed her feet on the ground.

"Bonjour!" yelled Esmerelda, her sparkling eyes whipping around to smile at the approaching couple. "Salutations on your Ranna!"

"Lisha vo, Esmerelda," Odesha replied happily sitting on her distinctive rock to watch the glowing lights. Kunchok stood, arms crossed, watching the pirate with narrowed eyes, not able to trust the witch, remembering the things she had kept from Odesha.

Esmerelda wrinkled her nose at him, sticking her tongue out. Kunchok just shook his head at her strangeness. Esmerelda remarked, "The sky celebrates your union. See the colors swirling matching your auras? Oh wait. You can't see those.

Anyways, that's what these colors are." Esmerelda lifted her arm, running it over waves as if an artist painted. "I must leave you now. They have made the choice, now it is up to you to get through the forest. I am going to commandeer Dek's home while you are gone." She laughed uproariously at this, clutching her sides as if she knew something they didn't. Odesha blinked her eyes trying to figure out her humor, but she just didn't understand.

"Where did the storm come from?" Odesha asked. She knew Esmerelda had an idea of the source of the storm.

Esmerelda sighed, drawing shapes beside her in the snow. "The storm has been building for many, many years. Before you were born. There has been enough blood spilt to create a vast amount of magic. The person responsible hides in the darkness and I haven't been able to draw them out. It aims to infect the rest of the land, seeking ways to spread its menace, through creatures or people alike. Sashi became entranced by its wiles getting lost in the snow one day. It was only a whisper in her ear, but it was enough to secure her loyalty. You were right, Odesha. The bloody tears. They show the sickness. I fear the next step it will take to spread." She finished with a sigh, erasing her drawings she had made in the snow.

Odesha asked softly, "Will I see you again?"

Esmerelda smiled, a sadness entering her eyes. "I said once I had no one. But you are inside my heart, along with your siblings, never forget that, sweet Odesha." Esmerelda's smile changed, becoming cunning and sharp. "You still owe me a boon, smol. Look, a cow beast!" She screamed this, pointing behind Odesha and Kunchok. He turned, grabbing his sword from his back to face the menace, while Odesha jumped from her rock to defend the group, but the snow was undisturbed. The wind gently howled with the emptiness around them.

"I don't see anything!" called Odesha, turning back to ask the witch what she had seen, but she was gone. The colors continued to swirl over the empty cliff, but this time a swirl of orange encircled them as if in an embrace, fading away in the distance.

Odesha sighed and motioned for Kunchok to sheath his sword. Esmerelda had given them the information she wanted them to have, nothing more, but Odesha wondered if Esmerelda knew more than she was letting on. It sounded like the storm was going to be a menace to everyone. They had to warn her father.

Kunchok sighed, shaking his head. The witch was a confusing mess of information. He would report what he had heard to Dek, but now it was time to enjoy the lights with his mate. He held out his hands, Odesha taking his hand with a smile. He led her to their rock, settling in to enjoy their last time with the lights. She snuggled in his fur, gently stroking him. The cold still didn't bother her now-warm heart, but it felt good to be close to Kunchok.

"Kunchok promise Odesha wedding." He stressed the last word, having practiced it in his hut, wanting to be together in both his way and hers.

Odesha smiled. "We can wait until we get settled. It is going to be a lot of stress on the tribe when they arrive at Antiqua. The different way of living, introducing the men to the mines, and the people to greet. Their wedding could wait until a later time, it didn't matter to her. She felt married to him in her heart. Kunchok just nodded his head, but inside he was already planning for the time when he could stand in front of her people and call her his in their way. Odesha moved around restlessly. Kunchok turned her chin in his hand to face him, looking at her face. "Odesha?"

"Make love to me under the lights, Kunchok," she whispered achingly. This would be their last time here and she wanted to treasure the memory. His long ears swiveled, trying to catch the noises in the distance. "Safe," he murmured, unfastening the top plates, letting them fall to the side. Odesha hesitated, spreading her legs over his. His cock was already hard, straining towards her. She leaned forward to place her lips on his, moving slowly, treasuring this feeling he caused in her. This was love. She felt it pulsing all around them. She placed his tip on her entrance, moving down him, savoring the sensation. Kunchok groaned, his head falling back at the sweet torture. She finally seated herself to the hilt, moving her hips back and forth. The tingling inside her grew, their pace increasing together until their release hit them both. Their cries flowed around them, echoing in the lights, forever memorialized by the promise of their love.

CHAPTER 17

The decision to leave the ice for Antiqua sent a shock wave through the community. The yeti gathered provisions in the two days their chief gave them. They stocked their supplies on sleds used to carry large items. Provisions were stored, while shops closed. The yeti's hope for a better future was bright as they worked together to tear apart their home and move to the plentiful land promised to them. Kunchok had a lot of cloth and weapons in his home. Odesha only took what they needed. Kunchok placed many of his weapons on a separate sled for the hunters if needed.

The day for travel arrived. Kunchok packed the sled, making sure their belongings were secured tightly. Dek's sled sat beside Kunchok's and Halana and Boni's. Halafren was helping his father, to the surprise of Halana. They hadn't spoken in a long time, she had explained.

Boni hurried to the leaders and reported, "Tribe ready chief." A sense of calm rushed over the group. They looked to their leaders, waiting for the signal to move. The children were even silent, knowing the great journey they planned. It wouldn't be bad for a smaller group, but this was an entire tribe moving as one through a dangerous place.

Dek pulled the straps around his shoulders. He looked to Kunchok, waiting for his signal, and nodded. A battle cry sounded with a flick of Kunchok's wrist, alerting the others the long trek had begun.

The pace was slow across the fresh snow. They had to make multiple stops to feed the people and rest. The elders were especially having a hard time, but they pushed on, determined. Dek called for the tents to be set up to rest for the night far enough from the orik forest to not be detected. They would face a great threat ahead of them tomorrow. The birds would hear the large party advancing through their territory, causing the entire tribe to be in great danger. The orik were starving and would prey on the young to the old.

Odesha stood far away from the people, pondering the dark forest waiting for them.

The next day would be daunting with the orik patrolling the wooden trees. There were no leaves to hide the massive party of people. There was no way to hide the tribe.

Odesha froze at that thought. Hide…there was a way! She scrambled to find Kunchok and Dek to tell them of her plan. They would only have one chance in a stolen moment to make it work, but it was worth a try.

The yeti were working on securing the tent hide with wooden stakes, when she burst through the clearing. Kunchok looked at her in concern. She was breathless in her excitement, panting with her words, frantically trying to explain. "I know how we hide from the king birds!"

Kunchok smiled at his mate, her clever mind continuing to surprise him. "Kunchok tell Dek king bird land no safe. Odesha plan?"

Odesha quickly explained her plan she had come up with, earning nods of approval from Dek and Kunchok. The battle could change in their favor if everything turned out the way it should.

As long as she could get the one on the other side to help. She had always been so independent. Strong-willed. Dangerous. It was going to be a task to make her see it Odesha's way.

Kunchok drove the stake deeper into the ground, distracting Odesha.

"I'm going to gather some food for the tent. It looked like it's about ready. Do you need any help?" Kunchok nodded in agreement, his muscles straining as he maneuvered the strong hide. "No help. Storm come next moon. Tribe leave first light." Kunchok nodded in the distance. Odesha squinted, trying to see a storm coming in the distance, but clear skies hovered as far as she could see.

"How do you know?"

Kunchok paused to think, shrugging slightly, "Feel storm inside." He thumped his chest with his fist, turning back to drive another stake. Interesting. She didn't know yeti could tell when a storm was about to come. Odesha hoped the storm didn't bring more creatures. They didn't need another problem on top of the orik.

Odesha hurried to the middle of the camp, Halana and Fanni expertly sorting food for the rest of the tribe. Boni attempted to steal meat from a clay plate. Halana caught him, swatting him with her wooden spoon on his backside. He yelped in surprise at the light smack, turning to his new mate with a questioning look. She laughed at his discomfort, shooing him away to help with the tents.

Odesha smiled, gathering up Kunchok's dinner. "Mate behaving Halana?" She wiggled her eyebrows.

Halana snorted in response. "Boni eat much. Halana good cook."

Odesha laughed. "Kunchok said there is a storm coming tomorrow. We are leaving early if you can spread the word during dinner. We will have to move quickly. Anything heavy needs to be left behind. When we make it through king bird land, we have to pass over the mountain peak. Then we will be home."

"Big storm come. Air feel different. Odesha eat?"

Odesha shook her head, blushing, and replied, "Ah. Kunchok and I are going to eat inside our tent tonight."

Halana smiled brightly. "Halana happy Odesha happy."

"Odesha happy too." She had finally found her balance between ice and fire and could look forward to a long life.

The worry about joining Freyja in the ice garden was gone.

Clearing her throat, Halana remarked, "Horm talk Halana. Halafren." Odesha gasped.

"What did he say?!"

"Horm say sorry treat young wrong. See Sashi evil. Wrong Boni. Happy Halana." Halana had lost her sad look that she carried around. It was mixture between being with Boni and having her father's blessing, Odesha was sure of it.

Odesha held her arms out, hugging the larger yeti to her. "I'm so happy you are at peace, Halana."

Halana returned to feeding the tribe, the long line forming. There was a lot of help from other yeti that joined in.

Odesha hurried back to the tent, carrying meat for Kunchok to eat. He had worked hard hauling their sled. Kunchok was on his knees placing feathered hide on the ground for them to keep warm during the night when she entered, but he didn't look up from his task. He scented his mate approaching and asked, "Odesha eat?"

A rustle of fabric sounded through the tent. Odesha stood in the doorway, naked, a plate held in her hand as she walked towards him. Her long white hair swished across her back, her pink nipples hard in the cold air.

Kunchok gulped, "Odesha no eat."

Odesha smiled shyly. "In my home, the women serve the men if they are interested in mating with them." Kunchok's fur flared in response, his gaze heating with lust. He tilted his head to the side, exposing his neck. "Male serve woman?"

Odesha's eyes locked on to his neck as she licked her lips fleetingly, the mating mark prominent when Kunchok exposed the area. His smile turned savage at the small gesture, growling softly, used to teasing Odesha. She was feisty when she wanted something.

"Odesha hungry?" he rumbled. She nodded her head, the breath leaving her chest quickly as her need increased.

"Come." Kunchok ordered, opening his arms wide, his great shoulders almost the length of the tent. Odesha walked slowly to the great yeti balancing the plate in her hands. His arms enfolded her as she held up a small piece of meat. His mouth opened, his sharp teeth gently taking it from her. She raptly watched his mouth while he continued to chew the rest of the food. Their eyes occasionally clashed, the tension in the room steadily rising as their needs took precedence.

Suddenly, Kunchok lashed forward to grasp Odesha's nipple between his teeth. She gasped, small tremors wracking her body as he gently sucked. The empty plate fell on the soft feathers while Kunchok devoured her gently. He leaned back to look in her eyes, "Kiss?" Their lips met as the fire inside her grew, tongues dueling for dominance. Kunchok pushed her to the feathers. Her hips spread in invitation. His heavy cock, extending out from his furred legs, gently pushed inside her. She hissed at the invasion, raking her nails down Kunchok's back. He growled deeply as he shoved forward, spearing her on his cock completely. The snarls and growls increased until they were both mindless, their bodies moving quickly to find completion. He looked down at his mate, her eyes lost at the pleasure they both shared.

"Bite Odesha. Feed."

Odesha's hands reached around Kunchok's head, lightly holding the soft white locks as she pulled him forward, whispering in his ear, "I love you." She sank her teeth deeply inside his exposed neck. He roared his release, pounding in her tight sheath as she took what he gave, whimpering her own release when her body clamped down tightly. Kunchok's arms gave out as he fell to his elbow, trying not to crush her smaller body.

Kunchok lifted his head from Odesha's beating heart. She gently stroked her claws through his fur. "What Odesha say?"

She smiled and replied, "I said I love you. Vo lo cos suti ba suta."

He nuzzled her neck, repeating the vow, "Kunchok love Odesha. Vo lo cos suti ba suta." He rolled over, pulling Odesha on top of him as they snuggled deep into the feathers.

"Odesha brother accept Kunchok?" he asked bluntly, running his claws down her side gently. He worried about their differences once they arrived in Antiqua. She had described her half-brother as a painfully blunt, harsh man who took his job as future king seriously, ruling without the crown.

Odesha shrugged, replying quietly, "It is hard to tell what brother thinks or what mood he is in. It changes so frequently. He is kind to Saphira."

"Brother no kind Odesha?" he asked, watching her eyes closely in case she tried to hide the truth. He didn't believe she would lie to him, but family was different when you were looking from the outside to describe a situation.

"He…tolerates me. I guess I've never opened up to him like I did my sister. For a while, she was all I had." Odesha yawned, burrowing deeper into her covers.

"Sleep," Kunchok whispered. They had forever to speak about her family, but tonight they needed to rest for the coming storm.

CHAPTER 18

The next day the sleds were packed early, the children roused from sleep. They held tightly to their parents in the white snowy field, apprehensive about the dark forest they had been warned about through their lives. The group reached the tree line of the orik forest. Kunchok, Dek, and Odesha stood in front of their people, shielding them from the harsh screams of the orik carrying on the wind. They were lucky to not see any flying around them. Breathing in deeply, Odesha braced for the hard battle ahead. The storm was creeping forward in the far distance, so they still had time.

Freyja give them strength. Let her see reason to help.

The weight of the bloodstone felt heavy in the

cold day. Odesha grasped it tightly, pulling it from underneath her gown, brushing the cold frost from the etched inscription on the silver face. In the harsh demonish language, she recited the words, calling forth the only one that could help them in their time of need.

The wind whipped Odesha's gown from her legs, tossing her hair into the air. Several yeti gasped, falling to their knees in prayer, whispering they were angering the spirits of the forest. The shape of a woman molded in front of Odesha as if spewing from the earth. The form solidified as the face of her sister came into view.

Vashti had arrived.

Vashti's form pieced itself back together. She had been training and was about to select her weapon when she had felt the pull take her. It had been shocking, seeing her hands disappear from her body. The faces around her were horrified. Vashti's shocking golden eyes locked with Odesha's, her golden hair arranged in a severe bun. Her loose black pants tangled with the wind, giving her an otherworldly appearance. A lone flame was stitched on her breast.

Vashti stood confused in the snow, eying her sister, and said with a gruff voice, "We thought you dead, sister."

Odesha's eyes watered with tears and rushed to embrace her twin. "We don't have much time to talk, Vashti."

She released her hold and grasped Odesha's hands urgently, asking, "Where are you and how did you call me to you?"

"Across the mountains from Antiqua, crossing into orik lands to reach home. I have to take this group through dangerous territory. Large carnivorous birds guard the skies." Odesha indicated the frightened people behind her and the forest in front of them. Kunchok stood firmly at her side giving her the confidence she needed.

Vashti's eyes tightened. "You bring these people home?" The suspicions in her heart were hard to break. She didn't trust many.

"Yes, yes. I don't have time to explain right now. Have the castle at Antiqua prepared. Send word to father. I'm better, Vashti, truly. I found my fire." She removed her hand from Vashti and clasped Kunchok's tightly, earning a fond look from her mate.

Vashti eyebrows rose. The large male beside Odesha was intimidating. It surprised her that Odesha had let him close enough to speak with her. The story of how they met would be interesting to hear. "You found your spirit as well it seems. I will have everyone await you at the castle," Vashti promised solemnly. She was happy for Odesha, truly she was.

"You never believed Mother's words about the fire inside," Odesha recalled, secretly happy that Vashti had agreed so quickly.

Vashti looked away, explaining, "I may have been harsh when it concerned Mother. Maybe she had another reason. But let's discuss what I learned when we have more time together." She shrugged dismissively, giving Odesha a sheepish smile. Vashti owed her an apology.

Odesha tugged her towards the forest, indicating where Kunchok had decided to enter. Vashti nodded her head, clasping her hand tightly, beginning to chant. Closing her eyes, Odesha joined with Vashti, reciting the words needed to turn the very air to do their bidding. The fog they called forth drifted through the trees, sheltering the traveling party from being seen by the orik. Dek released the call to move forward, the tight-knit people walking together cautiously through the trees. They ended their chant together, embracing each other to say goodbye.

"You never did say how you called me here, Odesha." Vashti's nails tightened slightly on Odesha's arm, sending a sliver of apprehension racing through her.

Odesha cleared her throat. "I received the bloodstone with the letter you sent wishing me well on my trip to Antiqua. Don't you remember sending it?"

Vashti shook her head, turning away quickly, trying to hide her worry. She released Odesha when Kunchok started to growl at her. A healed cut she received weeks ago pulsed. A push at the market in Romule with a bloody spot on her arm seemed like nothing to worry about, but now she wondered who else had her blood and what they planned to do with it.

Odesha watched her twin closely, seeing the slight wince of worry race through her eyes. She whispered, "Do you have more enemies now?"

Vashti shook her head, muttering back, "Not any more than usual." Vashti stared out into the snow in thought as her hands began to fade from view. Odesha noticed the quick fade, ripping the bloodstone from around her neck, extending a fang to prick her thumb, and pressing the bleeding digit over the seal. Vashti needed her now, there was no doubt. Her concern over the situation was obvious.

Odesha murmured the promise to the stone quickly, placing it around Vashti's neck. "If you don't see a sign of me by tomorrow…"

Vashti placed a finger over her mouth grimly.

"You will come home, I know it. Even if I have to hunt the bastard who is using us."

Odesha shivered, feeling pity for the person that stole her sister's blood as her body faded from view. Vashti had fire blazing in her veins, ready to scorch the world with her defiance. No one would stand in her way when she set her mind on something she wanted. Odesha turned back to the forest. Kunchok calmly waited at the tree line now that Vashti was gone. She ran to his side and helped heft the heavy sled, moving as silently as possible in the woods. Visibility was skewed, but hunters surrounded the group, helping to lead the people on the path they took on their frequent hunts. An occasional call from an orik peppered the air, but they seemed to stay over the top of the trees to stay far from the fog. It was as if they feared what they couldn't see. Odesha knew how they felt.

Black clouds floated across the trees, churning quickly, pushing fast over the tribe's heads as if searching for something. Kunchok grunted, nodding his head to the sky, alerting Odesha. She nodded back, watching the menacing clouds boil and push, trying to reach their chosen destination, wherever that would be. They didn't move as if normal clouds did, continuing to grow as if taking baby steps in a new world it had discovered. She could only hope the monsters it brought stayed in the dark and away from her people. The tribe was safe, concealed in the fog, hidden beneath the orik. They pushed on to join the rest of the group, hoping they were moving fast. The fog wouldn't last forever, especially now that Vashti was gone.

Dek sent out a muffled call, gathering the tribe together when they reached the edge of the fading trees, the mountain beginning its high peak. Once gathered, they continued their march together in an ordered fashion, the fog fading from the trees behind them, relieved of its burden. The calls from the orik were distant behind them, the danger from the giant birds in the air past. Odesha couldn't believe the success of her plan. Vashti must have been growing stronger to command this skill.

Boni had scouted ahead and called for Dek, alerting him he had found somewhere for the tribe to stop for the night. He had stepped up as a hunter, using the advice Kunchok and Dek had been giving him. Halana puffed up her chest with pride at her mate's scouting ability. Odesha spotted Halana, standing by Fanni, helping keep track of the young children while their parents rested. Fanni had, thankfully, left her brew of loma behind and was taking charge in true chief-like fashion. She was stepping up to help Dek shoulder the burden of the large group. Everyone was helping and it showed.

"No tribe lost king bird land Kunchok," Boni's messy appearance seemed relaxed as he reported his findings to his leader.

Kunchok grunted in acknowledgment, smacking Boni on the back. "Set tent." Boni nodded, hurrying away to his sled to obey his orders without argument. This would be their last night in this dangerous land and he wanted to make sure the tribe was secure.

Kunchok found a spot well-guarded by several rocks. He moved to secure their own tent to ready for the long night ahead. They were exposed and he knew it, but there was no other option. It was either here, the mountain, or the forest. It didn't leave them many options.

"My heart, I'm going to see if the food's been prepared and check on Fanni and Halana to see if they need help," Odesha called out.

Kunchok looked around, assessing the danger, finding none, and replied, "Yell loud Odesha need Kunchok. No safe." He pointed to the ground. She nodded apprehensively, walking towards the edge of the camp, keeping an eye out to monitor the hidden shadows. The darkness was starting to creep over the camp and Dek had ordered no fire to keep the orik from finding them. Everyone was on edge waiting for one to come from the sky. But that wasn't what they should fear.

CHAPTER 19

Halana directed the hungry tribe to the feeding area that she had set up. The meat was separated in clay bowls for the women to hand out to the working men patrolling and helping with the tents. They fed the children, quieting them when they became unruly or sad. It was tense throughout camp and the children could feel it.

Odesha hurried to help hand out food. She said, "Halana, I'm sorry we strayed from the group and caused you worry. My sister and I were catching up while I had time with her."

Halana smiled, replying, "Odesha same face sister."

"I was thankful she helped us. Yes, we are twins but different. My sister is the fierce one in our family. She is strong and curvy, while I'm just skin and bones. That's how I escaped the orik. Surely they wouldn't want to eat bones?" Odesha smiled, trying to lighten Halana's somber mood. Her ears were swiveling, a tell-tale sign she was checking for danger and trying not to let Odesha worry.

Halana set another clay plate on the small wooden table, asking, "Odesha no think sister help?"

Odesha sighed. "Vashti can be…harsh at times. She turned her back on our mother's teachings, refusing to acknowledge her while I followed them to the very last word. But now I see that Vashti was right on many things she argued. I just haven't had the chance to tell her yet. But I will next time I see her."

Halana wiped her hands on a hide cloth, turning to pat Odesha on the back as they finished handing out the last ration. They had saved two plates for Boni and Kunchok for later. "Odesha tell sister home one moon."

Odesha smiled, hoping Halana was right. Clearing her throat, Odesha said, "I never gave you my sorrow over Sashi's death."

Halana shook her head, muttering, "Sashi no friend. Evil. Jealousy change Sashi. Glad Odesha."

"I'm glad I'm here too." She patted the yeti on the back of her soft hand, smiling gently. Halana was a good friend.

"Odesha take food Kunchok," Halana ordered gruffly.

Odesha paused in taking the food, asking, "Halana, do you think it's early to be so dark?"

Halana frowned, sniffing the air, whispering, "Storm."

A low growl in the darkness alerted Odesha that they weren't alone, making the two women stop in their tracks. The sound magnified as if it came from every direction, many sinister sounds raised in chorus around them. The storm had arrived, hidden in the fading light, releasing the monsters it held in the deep.

Terror grasped Halana by the throat, causing her panicked breaths to escalate. Odesha didn't seem to have the same reservations. She let out a loud scream, alerting the guards.

The hunters ran to protect the tribe, bracing themselves around the group in a circle. They pulled weapons free from their sheaths to ready for the battle. Kunchok heard the yell, his blood turning to ice at the terror in Odesha's scream. He wouldn't let anything hurt his mate, letting out a roar in challenge to the thing that had frightened Odesha. He was coming, he promised her. He wouldn't lose her when he had just found her.

Odesha put her back to Halana's to keep an eye

on the beasts hidden in the snow, the glow of the eyes glistening lifeless with bloody tear tracks furrowing their face. The skin hung down in giant rolls as if something had been stuffed inside the body that wasn't made to fit. The droopy eyes looked calm, the teeth and tusks standing out in a snarl. It was startling to see. She heard the stomp of feet as the cow beasts emerged, attacking the hunters, rushing through the snow to ambush the tribe. They weren't like the first cow beast she had encountered. That cow beast was in the throes of the sickness that gripped it, fighting for his life. These were lifeless puppets being told to kill.

One beast stood silently inside the protective clouds surrounding them, watching the carnage without movement. The same soulless beast Esmerelda had fought in the snow the first day Odesha had met her. Odesha kept her eyes on the cunning one, trying not to alert it that she was watching.

The puppeteer waited for its victory hidden in the storm. Inside lurked a powerful being capable of using the skin of the dead animals for its own purpose.

"I'm going for the large beast over there," Odesha whispered to Halana, handing her friend an ice spear she had quickly formed to defend herself. The pain never came with forming the ice, which Odesha was thankful for. She didn't need the distraction. With Kunchok's blood pumping through her, she felt invincible.

Halana shook her head with worry, trying to convince her friend not to go. She could sense how menacing the thing inside was. It radiated a black magic pulsing with the blood of its victims. Halana warned, "Beast evil. Odesha no safe."

"If we kill it the attack will stop. Someone is controlling these beasts through the eyes of that one," Odesha pointed out. If the puppeteer couldn't see its puppets, it would drag them back into the storm like last time.

Odesha gripped her pointed ice spear tightly, trying to keep the beast in the corner of her eye while she made her way to the side of it, avoiding cow beasts charging towards her and hunters swinging swords. The skin hanging from their faces impeded their vision. The smell of rotten flesh flowed from them, clogging her senses.

Whirling in panic at a soft noise behind her, thinking a beast was attacking from behind, Halana stood before Odesha shivering bravely, clutching her spear.

Odesha frowned, ordering, "It's dangerous. Go back to the tribe so the hunters can protect you.

Please, Halana, I don't want to see anything happen to you!"

"No! Halana help Odesha," the yeti stated firmly, not budging an inch, yelling out her denial. It was the first time she had raised her voice to Odesha, but if something happened to her furless friend, she would never forgive herself.

A scream of death pierced the air from a tribe member. The hunters roared in fury at hearing their fallen brethren, their great arms swinging swords. The skin of the cow beasts fell to the ground easily with a swipe of the sword, but the sheer amount of them was hard to overcome.

"We've got to hurry before it sends more!"

Odesha moved swiftly to the side of the beast, taking it by surprise. The head lolled on its nape, trying to see the danger. She threw the ice spear towards the drooping head of the beast. It moved back, bending in half to escape the shard. Its head flopped forward, looking at her as if annoyed by her interference. The animal took off running in a loping sprint towards her. The skin gathered itself up to help propel it forward awkwardly. Odesha scurried back on her hands and knees in panic, trying to escape before it trampled her. She didn't have time to grow another spear. A large yeti arm descended over the beast's head, stabbing an ice shard through the top. The shard pierced deep, the animal stopping its advance towards Odesha. Halana fell back in shock, scuttling away from the creature she had just stabbed. The oddly shaped skin melted around the glowing eyes, staring menacingly at Odesha. It glowed brightly, its last moments, to memorize the face of the being responsible for its defeat. And it would remember.

A yeti sword swung in a downward arc across the neck of the animal, narrowly missing the two women. The head was torn from the creature's body. Kunchok stood over them breathing heavily, cape torn from his shoulder as blood flowed down from deep cuts in his armor. He had fought four cow beasts, killing them as quickly as possible to reach Odesha. He had felt a battle rage take over him he had never felt before. He was mindless, hacking and slashing through the animals attacking.

As soon as the creature's head fell from its body, the cow beasts around them dropped to their bellies. Their skin lay in the snow not moving, the glow of their eyes gone. The glowing strings of the puppeteer become evident, pulling the cow beasts back to their dark hole in the storm. The dark clouds disappeared in a swirl of wind and snow, rising from the ground. Their evil presence was gone.

Several tribe members yelling for help became

evident. Kunchok checked Odesha for wounds, running his hands up and down her body checking for blood when he was the one flowing with it.

"I'm fine! Help the tribe, Kunchok. Oh, great Freyja, you are bleeding!" Odesha cried out, mopping at the blood dripping from his armor. She checked the wounds, but they were shallow. He brushed her hand away, replying, "Kunchok heal fast. Help tribe." The shouts of distress were increasing.

Odesha turned her attention to Halana once she made sure Kunchok's bleeding stopped, asking, "Halana, are you hurt? Can you stand? I can smell blood across the tribe, we need to see who needs help." Odesha rushed to help her up, dusting the snow from her body. She didn't notice any wounds.

"Halana good. Help tribe. Boni help tribe… Boni?!" Halana ran off, shouting for her mate, but she didn't hear him among the voices.

A head popped up from a fallen yeti, holding pressure on a wound, calling back to Halana. Odesha breathed a sigh of relief that he was okay. She didn't know what the two would do without each other. Kunchok grasped her hand, running to find Dek and Fanni while checking on anyone they passed. Dede cried softly in Fanni's arms at the noise and chaos.

Dek still had his bloody sword in one hand, issuing orders.

"Kunchok, six dead. Much wounded," Dek yelled, moving towards them. Kunchok nodded to the hunters gathering around him. He ordered them to help the fallen tribe members. They were used to staunching wounds and healing cuts while hunting.

"Cow beasts come where?" Dek wondered aloud.

Odesha answered, "From the storm that's been chasing us. Someone very powerful controls the beasts, using their skins to attack. When Kunchok cut down the skin it hid in, it pulled the other beasts back inside the storm. That's where your food source went. The cow beasts were taken away to be used against you this whole time."

"Tribe wonder where food go. Why attack tribe?" Dek shook his head in disgust at the waste of it all.

Odesha thought hard on this, remembering Esmerelda's warning that if they stayed, they would all die. She replied, "Because the mage behind all of this wanted you to be the skins it could use. Your strength is superior to most races and your intelligence sets you apart from the rest of the beings on the ice. Did you notice the orik when the storm passed over the trees? They hid from it. They knew what it is capable of."

Kunchok growled, "Monster kill tribe."

Dek nodded his head, remarking, "Tribe left good time."

Odesha realized he was more right than he thought, muttering, "Yes, almost like we were led here. Sashi said when she died "the sky will use me no longer" Sashi wasn't trying to kill Kunchok that day. She was trying to kill me. Because without me, you wouldn't have left. You would still be out in the snow. The sky was using her. The mage in the shadows used Sashi. Don't you remember the blood coming from her eyes? She was sick. Like the cow beast that had attacked on the first day. But they weren't dead yet like these creatures."

Without Esmerelda's warnings and help, they would still be out in the snow, waiting. The tribe would've been killed and taken in the storm. Esmerelda had said she couldn't see them anymore, but maybe that was because she was looking for someone, and not the storm itself. She knew who it was that was doing this.

Dek hurried away to check on more tribe members, calling, "Dek think. Rest. Some injuries no big. Hunters bury tribe in snow. Storm no get tribe," He paused while leaving. "Horm gone Odesha."

She placed her fingertips to her lips at the shock, whispering, "No…poor Halana. I need to find her and see if she is alright."

Kunchok wrapped his arm around Odesha, asking, "Odesha good?" She nodded, thankful they were alive and unhurt.

"I'm sad for Halana and the other tribe members loss." She looked around. "Is Halana with her father?"

He shook his head. "Halana and Halafren say bye. Father gone. Halana with Boni. Tribe rest."

She sent a prayer to Freyja to watch over the fallen tribe members when they entered their tent to rest before the final day of hiking. They would hold each other tightly tonight, knowing their near loss and thinking of the dangers lurking in the night. The storm had suffered a loss this night and had withdrawn to lick its own wounds, but it would be back one day. She only hoped to be back in Antiqua by then.

CHAPTER 20

The day began, the happiness diminished. The somber mood and loss of their tribe members caused them to move slowly like a mourning party. Odesha hurried from her tent to find Halana standing beside her sled hugging Halafren.

"Halana, I'm so sorry for your father," Odesha said gently when they parted. Halafren returned to his own sled, securing it tightly.

Halana nodded her head in thanks, a lone tear falling from her face. "Father no good. No bad. Halana miss. Glad Boni. Glad friends." Odesha hugged her furry body to her.

"You saved us all yesterday, Halana. Your father would be proud." Halana smiled. She had felt courage for the second time yesterday, the first was her Ranna day.

This was the day the tribe would reach the other side of the mountain by traveling up the mountain pass the hunters had spotted. It was a shortcut carved in the side. Dek bellowed the order to begin the trek and the group marched along with a brisk step eager to reach their new home. The glistening icicles and frozen trees were beautiful in the low light through the path. The frozen stone shined brightly, giving the tribe a sense of peace. A light after the storm. The trek was long and hard, the tribe stopped frequently to rest and regroup the stragglers. By the end of the day, they reached the end of the pass and could see the very top of the castle turrets in the distance. They were moving downhill now. At times the slippery slope caused a fall or two. The tribe laughed when they called back that they were unhurt, enjoying the ice.

A shout from the bottom of the mountain sounded through the pass. The hunters became alert, drawing their swords from their backs, bracing in a protective stance. Odesha called for Dek to stop. The voice that had shouted was familiar, but she needed to hear it again. The thudding of hooves became evident, the shadows from the ground came into view. A face peered up from his horse, noticing the group. Her personal guard sent with her to Antiqua straddled the horses at the bottom of the mountain, calling to her.

Captain Philo shouted from the front, "Princess Odesha? My lady! We received a pigeon from Vashti on where to find you!" The tension leached from her body; she gave a sigh of relief. Her guard would help protect them.

"Yes! Yes! I hear you! I have brought many people with me on my journey. Stand down as we emerge from the pass. We shall meet you there at the bottom, Captain." Dek nodded to her, the straps tight on his shoulders. She gripped Kunchok's hand nervously. They were almost home. The tribe marched down the pass, excitedly talking of their arrival to their new home. A loud cheer rang in the air when the guards spotted their princess, celebrating her return. Odesha called out to the guard, "These people are honored guests to Antiqua. Please help guard them as you would me." Her orders were followed.

The guards acknowledged her orders, fanning out to help with children, hefting sleds from weary travelers. The walk to the castle was much quicker with their help, cutting down the time it took to make it. Darkness was falling on the land when the large group reached the inner gates of the castle. The yeti looked around in astonishment at the workmanship of the castle, the large gargoyle-like demons carved in the stone watching over their domain. The rough points of their skin frozen in stone were menacing in the fading light.

Some of the yeti were so weary they lay down to rest on the snow in the courtyard. Dek and his family stayed with the tribe, giving a nod to Kunchok to approach the castle with Odesha, letting him take charge of their well-being. On the steps of the castle, waiting silently, stood Prince Endemion and King Desmond. They were regal and tall, their black horns flared into the air. Endemion with his long black attire, matching his short hair, stood proudly beside father with a menacing presence. He reminded Odesha of the dark cats slinking in the Bijou forest she had seen in books, waiting for their prey to strike. Odesha glanced to her father, who stared hard at Odesha's hand clasped in Kunchok's. The king's hair fanned out from his face, sticking in all directions, his large clawed hand absently scratching his belly.

Suddenly the king let out a giant bellow of a laugh, sending a shock wave through the tribe at the loud sound. He lunged down the stairs to reach them, clasping Odesha in a tight hug, yelling, "Well look at you, little princess! You've got color to your cheeks and fire in your eyes. And you've gone and caught yourself an ice fey!"

Odesha was surprised, asking faintly, "Ice fey?!"

Confused, the king cleared his throat and repeated slowly, "The hairy man you won't let go of. I don't think I'm seeing things. What time is it, Endemion? "

Endemion shook his head, not bothering with a reply. Desmond had started drinking earlier in the day, causing problems in the castle again.

Annoyed, Odesha flailed in her father's arms. This made everyone around them chuckle. "I thought he was a yeti," she cried out, shielding her face in her hands.

At this, Desmond looked perplexed. "Now, you know there is no such thing as yeti. I thought I told you of the ice fey that ruled Antiqua before the vampires when you were younger."

"Yes, well, I am aware that there's no yeti, but what else was I supposed to call them? I vaguely remember you telling the story now that I think about it. Put me down, Father," Odesha sighed in exasperation. She was embarrassed for calling the noble ice fey yeti this entire time. They had once been the rulers over Antiqua, and she had studied them in the past. Great Freyja, she had even seen their relative in the hallway with the other rulers.

The king chortled and released Odesha from his arms. Landing with a thump on her feet, Odesha heard Endemion call her name. She turned to face him apprehensively. Odesha walked slowly up to her younger, stern-faced brother curtsying low to show her respect.

Father was called the jovial king. The laughing one. Prince Endemion was known as being harsh. His judgments rained hard over wrongdoers, his edicts heeded by all. Everyone knew that the prince was to be feared, a perfect contrast to the king.

A dark prince…for a light king…

"Well met, Prince Endemion," Odesha whispered to him softly.

He bowed stiffly, ordering Odesha to raise her eyes to his. The black of his eyes swirled dangerously when he pierced Odesha with them. It was hard to tell if he was in a pleasant mood or not. He looked around the tribe brought before him, lingering on Kunchok.

"Your trials over the mountain seem to have brought new faces to our doorstep, Princess Odesha."

Always so proper. But he was worried about something. She could feel it.

Odesha rose from her curtsy. "Yes, Prince. These people sheltered, protected, and fed me during my time away. I hope to explain the whole story to you in private, in hopes that they may st…"

His dark brow furrowed, eyes flashing to say, "You wish for them to stay here? Why?"

Clearing her throat, nervously holding his gaze, Odesha replied, "I am in love with Kunchok. I married him in their custom, which makes him your brother now."

Kunchok stood stiffly at her side, reaching out to grasp her hand in support. He looked at Endemion fearlessly and growled harshly at the man Odesha feared so much. "Love Odesha. Mine salt. Give Prince orik land." Odesha translated to the crowd, breathing a sigh of relief at this new ploy. She hadn't thought of the land. With Odesha's happiness and gain found, the Prince had no reason to say no to their union.

Endemion looked Kunchok up and down, crossing his arms across his thick chest. His eyes cleared of worry. The courtyard was eerily silent when Endemion ordered, "Come inside. Only you two for now."

They entered the cold throne room, the guards fanning out. Father laughed with the guards he brought from Merdi as he attempted to coax thick demon brew from the barrels in the corner of the room, oblivious to the tension. Endemion took over the proceedings.

Endemion spoke from his new perch on the throne, "I accept your offer of land and the claim to the Princess. She is my sister and a beloved princess, so you will treat her with respect. Or the consequences will be…painful. Do you understand me?" His sharp claws tapped a pattern on the raised arm rest, waiting for the fey's response. He had never met an ice fey before, but he was part woodland fey. In a way, they were similar.

Odesha translated, Kunchok nodding hard, raising his arm to beat on his chest loudly. He executed a bow like everyone had practiced in camp. Endemion raised a brow, bowing his head slightly in return at the good manners he displayed.

His face hardening, Endemion stated, "I have sent a pigeon to notify Gamble and Miravena of your return. They will arrive shortly. Kunchok, why would you want to reenter this land? The ice fey left Antiqua hundreds of years before the Blood War, wanting to find a new home through open waters on the ship your own people made. The stories tell of a prophecy foretold to them that they needed to leave Antiqua. But you return? It doesn't make sense."

Odesha translated, sensing Endemion's increased agitation. He wanted a reason as to why they wanted to return to their old lands. Did they wish to take back their lands and kill his own people? Or was it another reason he hadn't thought of yet?

Kunchok hesitated, replying honestly, "Tribe want home. No food tribe ice. Enemy fight tribe ice. Ship?"

Odesha clarified, "With the dwindling food source they had no choice but to return." She turned to Kunchok. "A ship is a giant home you float on waterways. It has a wooden circle that moved the ship back and forth."

Kunchok shrugged. "Dek home circle."

"Of course," Odesha muttered thinking back to the halls she had journeyed. They had seemed familiar when she first arrived. It was a large ship containing the rooms of the people it transported. "Dek's home is the ship frozen in the ice. They had departed from Antiqua only to freeze on their journey." She reminded herself to tell Endemion of the mysterious storm in private. The guards may be his hand-picked, but they still had wagging tongues.

Endemion shook his head, his black claws pinching his nose, trying to control his temper at the convoluted story. They weren't being completely honest, that much he could tell. And the fey had mentioned an enemy. He didn't have the time or patience for this today, his mood was as dark as his cloak he wore.

Endemion sat up abruptly when he reached his decision, ordering, "Kunchok, follow me."

Odesha nervously translated again and Kunchok nodded his head, following Endemion and his guards out of the throne room.

Looking to Father, Odesha noticed he had somehow procured a large chalice and climbed on top of a table to sing a bawdy song of a demon in a tower to his listening audience.

Well it looked like he wouldn't be any help. She only hoped Fanni wouldn't meet him yet.

Odesha hurried back outside to the courtyard to give the update to Dek. He nodded, shouting out the Prince's decision to the tribe.

He turned to Odesha, asking, "Where tribe stay?" She hadn't thought that far, looking around in thought, but Miravena and Gamble stood silently to the side waiting for their princess to notice them. She turned to pose the question to them, gesturing them forward, she called, "It's lovely to see you ag…"

"Oh, my lady!" Miravena babbled, throwing her arms around Odesha unceremoniously. Odesha stiffened in surprise when Gamble burst into tears, crying in his hands. His one piece of hair was slicked down from its usual pointy position on his head.

He shouted out, "We thought dat giant bird had dang gum gobbled you right up der on dat mountain top! Whole army sent but couldn't find a durn piece of yous to bury proper like!"

Odesha shushed them, patting Mira on the back to console them, "No, you both did your best in that situation. We have more mouths to feed and more hands to help. Let's start with dinner. Mira, you will have Fanni and Halana to work with. They're close friends of mine. Use hand signals since they can't speak our language. Gamble, your resources are going to be Boni and Dek. They are very friendly, but Dek is their chief. Let's speak about the mining tomorrow, not today, please. Mira, do you have any issues with the people I need to address today?"

"Yes, my lady. We have a child that is sickly. She needs the Reawakening as soon as possible. And I hope not to speak out of turn, my lady, but you look very well."

Wiggling out of Mira's arms, Odesha pinched her brow tightly to relieve the oncoming headache, replying, "Thank you. It will take time for the bath to fill during the night. Let's do the ceremony early in the morning so the child doesn't suffer."

Mira curtsied in acknowledgment, racing off to

find homes for the ice fey, notebook at the ready. Gamble sniffled again, staring up at Odesha with wide eyes.

"My lady. I musts tells yous bout the mines now! I don't means to speaks out of turn, but the salt. All of its was takens tos Romule on Vladeric's command. The profits have all being going to Romule!" His eyes well with fresh tears, the betrayal clear in his eyes.

"Why would Vladeric send the money to Romule?"

"Didn't you knows, my lady? Vladeric was a royal of some sorts, sitting mighty high in Romule."

"Great Freyja. I'll have to report this to Endemion. Thank you so much, Gamble." She had forgotten. Hadn't Vladeric warned her when she ordered his death? The report of Romule receiving all the salt profits was troubling. What could they need the money for? A new army? Was the Blood War to begin again?

She placed her hand on his arm to point him towards Boni and Dek. Gamble puffed his chest out proudly, strutting towards the two giants, gesturing where he wanted to lead them. They looked at him with raised brows, the skinny man's different-colored garb helping him stand out.

Odesha hurried back inside to make sure

Endemion was being cordial to Kunchok and report the findings of the profits. This was a serious matter.

The pictures of the old kings and queens stared down at her as she made her way through the hallways.

Odehsa felt a dark pull of magic flutter through the air. Endemion's voice spoke harsh demon tongue through a closed door. She sprinted towards the doorway, grasping the handle to pull urgently. The door opened. Kunchok grasped his head in his hands tightly, kneeling on the floor in front of Endemion.

Endemion continued, his black eyes bright red, holding a large book.

Dear Freyja, her brother was killing her husband.

Odesha screamed, racing towards Kunchok to help him.

Endemion gently shut the book, announcing, "A wedding gift to you both. Since he is linked to his people, I was able to give them the knowledge of our language. No more translating. It will take much less time. I don't seem to have a lot of that anymore." Endemion wasn't going to mention he had looked through Kunchok's memories while he was implanting the language. That would just be rude.

Odesha looked up to Endemion, bewildered at this kind offering.

She cleared her throat, replying hesitantly, "Gamble explained where the profits of the mines have been going. Vladeric ordered the salt to be sent to Romule. When I ordered his death, he mentioned being related to the royals there."

Endemion answered, "The King of Romule doesn't have any siblings as far as I know. His latest wife does have several siblings. I'll find out what Romule is up to." Another item to take up his time. And the list kept growing.

Turning, Endemion left the room, taking his dark presence with him without another word.

Kunchok turned to Odesha, "You can hear me speak now?" The halting tongue was easy to understand, the new words flowing through him. The knowledge coursed through him, this complicated language. He could express his feelings to his mate even better now, thankful for the Prince for giving him the gift.

"Well, yes, of course…" But he had spoken in the vampire tongue. He could speak to the people of Antiqua.

Brother might actually…care?

"Think Odesha's brother knows of monsters in

storm now. I could feel him reach into my mind. I saw events replayed as if reliving them."

Endemion didn't care, he wanted answers. That was the brother she knew. Take without asking.

Kunchok cleared his throat, looking at Odesha with concern. "Endemion told me of your curse Odesha. How do we fix it?"

Kunchok hadn't asked *if* they could fix it, Odesha took note of that right away.

"*You* broke my curse, Kunchok. I couldn't make you understand before Ranna, but the ice melted from my heart when you accepted me. I can't feel the pain anymore." Odesha began to laugh, rubbing her chest in joy. She realized that she now had a chance at life. The ice wouldn't take her now and she didn't have to join the ice garden. Kunchok sighed with relief.

"Let's go check on your people," Odesha replied. Now that the worry of her curse had passed, she didn't want to dwell on what Endemion may have seen in Kunchok's mind. That would be horrifying.

Kunchok stopped her from turning away, stating, "Our people."

"Yes. Our people." They were one now. The fey and the people of Antiqua mingled together. The miners ordered to take the day off to meet the new village members.

Mira and Gamble did well with their counterparts, rejoicing when they could understand each other. It had been by accident they had discovered they could speak to each other. One moment they were miming hand signals, the next they were speaking in full sentences.

Antiqua had many homes available for the couples. Only a handful of single fey were grouped in homes together. But they could always build more.

The late dinner they had was festive, a celebration planned for tomorrow. Fanni met the King, overjoyed that someone had her love for drink. The King was happy he had a new taste tester. Dek just shook his head at the merry pair as they sang to the crowd together the songs of their people. Endemion sat alone on the throne, gazing into the shadows, not attempting to be sociable as plans for the future grew in his overburdened head. Kunchok and Odesha sat with Boni and Halana discussing the future and their new home. This was the new Antiqua. Full of love, laughter, and family. Kunchok and Odesha retired early, heading to her old rooms.

"Odesha happy here?" Kunchok asked, admiring his small mate walking tiredly beside him. They had come so far together. From an orik forest where Odesha was buried in an avalanche, to the hall of Antiqua.

Odesha looked up at him to reply, "I felt cold when I first got here, torn from Vashti. The ice was taking me over and I was going to let it. I wasn't feeling much at all. But I think the tribe, especially you, brought me out of a shell I hadn't realized I was carrying around. I think the ice would have smothered me until I froze to death. And now I realize Father saw that when he sent me here. He was trying to give me a chance at life. This whole time I wonder if Father has been watching us closer than he let on. He may act like a carefree king, but he worried for us. Mother died when I was younger and had always warned Vashti and I not to find our fire. Because if your fire doesn't accept you, then it could mean your death. It made Mother crazed that her fire abandoned her and she jumped to her death."

Kunchok nodded his head. "Glad King sent Odesha here." They entered the rooms together, gazing at the large bed.

"I feel like we are getting married all over again," whispered Odesha shyly.

Kunchok placed a claw under her chin to raise her gaze to his, replying, "Kunchok mate Odesha every day if Kunchok could."

Odesha smiled at him. "Do you want to wash up before we go to bed?" A basin of water had been placed on the bedside table. If they wanted a full bath, they would have to summon help.

"No. Quick wash. Want Odesha in bed." Odesha giggled lightly, grabbing a washcloth to run over their bodies. Kunchok watched her with gentle eyes as she slowly moved lower, her breathing beginning to increase. He could tell her arousal was quickly growing. His hands gently pulled her tunic from her shoulder, exposing a breast. The pointed tip called to him as he gently sucked it into his mouth, causing her to moan. He smiled when she forgot to keep washing him and took the washcloth from her hand, quickly finishing washing. He wet it again to run it lovingly over her.

She moaned softly, running her fingers through his white fur. He tossed the cloth aside when done, turning his full attention to Odesha. Nipping at her lips, he slipped inside, running his tongue along hers when she opened her mouth. He lifted her in his arms, placing her on the bed. She gripped his fur tightly, moving him to his back as she ran her hands over his thick shaft stroking it softly. He groaned, tilting his head back, her soft hands causing him to harden even more as she leaned down, gently licking his tip. Cursing, he pulled her legs apart to enter her. He thrust inside quickly, muttering an apology at her gasp. Odesha began to rock her hips, moving quickly as the pleasure boiled inside her. Kunchok's hair fanning out, muscles bulging, was the last sight she saw before she closed her eyes on a scream, her orgasm ripping through her body while Kunchok let loose a loud bellow, the sheets tearing under his claws as his seed released in her tight sheath. Odesha fell forward to Kunchok's chest, gently breathing in his cool minty scent, feeling truly home at last.

CHAPTER 21

With a dawn of a new day, the people of Antiqua mingled, setting up the market. Odesha stared out the icy window in their room, watching the bustle. The ice fey and the miner families helped each other clear more space for their wares. Life was progressing. Kunchok rustled in bed behind her as he wakened for the day.

Kunchok asked roughly, "Does Antiqua look different since Odesha left?"

Odesha ran her finger over the dried blood trail she had left on the wall before leaving, replying to his question, "Everything is much brighter. The present and the future are something I look forward to now. With you by my side, I'm happy. I wish my sisters were here to enjoy it with me."

She looked behind her. Kunchok growled fiercely,

"Kunchok always be by Odesha's side." His eyes looked lighter with the knowledge his tribe would have food now. They had a place to call home. He had a family again.

Odesha sat on the side of the bed and said, "Come with me, love, it's time for the Reawakening. The poor child is suffering." She had explained the purpose of the ceremony during the late night with Kunchok while discussing their homes. He knew what had to be done to ease the child's sickness.

Kunchok stood, going to the wardrobe provided by the Prince, selecting loose clothing. No more armor unless they were under siege. He had never felt lighter. The heavy armor wasn't chafing him or weighing him down, but the protection had been needed at the time. They were safe here, their tribe protected in the high walls.

The ceremony robes swayed as they made their way down the hallway to the blood pool that Mira had ordered filled during the night. Mira waited inside, holding the towels patiently.

The family sat with their young son on a corner bench, his young face pale and gaunt. He was in pain and Odesha wanted to hurry to help.

Kunchok released her arm to stand at the side of the room, arms crossed. His shoulders stiffened, displaying his nervousness at this ritual that was strange to his culture. Odesha stepped gingerly in the pool, reaching her arms out to the young child. The family hurried forward, carrying him, to place him in her arms. She whispered to him, "What is your name, child?" This time she added a smile that came easily.

"Benye, my lady," he coughed quietly. She stroked Benye's hair back and gave him the same directions she had last given Evie, loudly enough that Kunchok and his family could hear and be at peace. Lowering them gently into the pool of blood, she completed the binding words of the ceremony. Life poured into the young boy. His eyes sparkled as the sickness left him. His body filled out with health.

Suddenly, Odesha felt a tingle in her hand. Looking down, the hand holding the back of Benye was disappearing. She realized what was happening and thrust the boy up to his parents to keep him safe. She attempted to climb out of the pool. Kunchok ran to her side and tried to reach her in panic, but a sharp pull made her lose her footing. She fell back into the blood. A large bubble engulfed her, pulling her deep where she couldn't escape. Odesha screamed, thrashing in the blood, trying to reach the surface. A splash disturbed the pool when someone jumped in. She felt herself being taken under when…

She was summoned.

The bloodstone pulled her away from Antiqua.

She had to answer the summons that called her, hearing the words in her mind that Vashti uttered to pull Odesha to her.

What felt like just moments later, Odesha's body returned to Antiqua. She regained her footing on the bottom of the pool.

The cool blood dripped down her body while steam poured from her skin.

She wiped her eyes, trying to see where she returned to. Kunchok roared in anguish on his knees, fur caked with blood as he swiped through the far side of the pool searching for her. Blood splattered the walls. Miravena stared at Kunchok in fear. Benye and his family were absent from the room. Endemion stood at the entrance, his eyes red with rage, glaring at Kunchok, his fists were clenched at his side.

She must have been gone longer than she thought.

Odesha cleared her throat loudly, drawing everyone's attention. Kunchok's haggard face lightened in relief at her sudden reappearance, jumping in the pool and enfolding her in his arms, letting out a long, drawn-out groan of misery. He whispered brokenly, "Thought blood swallowed Odesha."

Hugging him back, she reassured him, "Vashti had the bloodstone, remember? She summoned me."

Endemion walked to the edge of the pool, eyes fading to a cool black signaling his mood was calming. He asked mildly, "Vashti used a bloodstone? Is she on her way here then with Saphira?"

Glancing up to Endemion in apprehension at the news she was about to deliver, Odesha replied, "No, Prince. They are both far, far away from here. They were being held against their will and in extreme danger… And I'm not entirely sure if Vashti wants to be rescued…or not." Odesha was still confused about that part.

Endemion's eyes turned a menacing shade of red, heralding the storm coming for Vashti. Odesha would have to explain Saphira's situation before he left in a rage from the room.

"Vashti requested you retrieve Saphira first. She is busy trying to survive the trials of Baklan and wasn't sure where Saphira had been taken, only that they were both near the Bijou Forest when they were separated. They were both stolen from the pier trying to board Autum's ship."

Endemion clenched his hand, his voice lashing

like thunder across the room, "And where was Autum when this was going on?"

"Vashti said Autum was there when she fell but didn't see what happened to him. He could be dead for all she knows."

Endemion nodded, turning to leave the room. He would have to find Saphira, Vashti, and Autum in that order. They were his family. Desmond had fostered Autum from a young boy. They had grown up together and had the loss of their mothers in common and leaned on each other for support. He would find them all and bring them back.

The land would tremble beneath his rage if he didn't get them all back safely. It was a promise.

CHAPTER 22

Odesha strolled through the halls of Antiqua, looking for Miravena, having left Kunchok in bed to sleep. The scare of her Reawakening disappearance had taken a toll on him. He watched her constantly and it was slowing her down. There were many things to do since she had been gone so long. She had to check on the mining progress, check to see if the celebration was being planned to welcome the new tribe accordingly, and had to check on the people themselves. Not in that order, but she was racing around frantic trying to finish everything before the day was out.

Instead, she ran into the one person she didn't particularly want to. Turning a corner, she stumbled against a large body slouched in the hallway, sitting on his bottom.

Father.

Odesha approached him cautiously. The low moans he was emitting showed he had drunk too much the night before. Again.

She sat down beside him, eventually getting his attention. Resting her cheek against her folded knees, she asked quietly, "Why was Vladeric sent here?" Odesha had promised herself she would ask him the next time she saw him, and she wasn't going to miss this opportunity.

Desmond quit moaning and rubbed at his head. The silence stretched between them. He had never been one to talk with his children about the orders he had given or the past, but now seemed like a great time while he had a massive headache throbbing along his temples.

He grumbled, "That was a long time ago. Are you sure you want to know the truth?" His eyes remained closed against the candlelight. The flame was trying to stab him in his eye, he knew it, so he peeked an eye open to see her reaction cautiously. Odesha nodded tightly. Desmond's bushy eyebrows rose in surprise. His first daughter had always been the one to stay in the shadows, staying away from conflict or intrigue. This was a new development. Her time on the ice had truly brought her out of her shell.

Clearing his throat, Desmond tried sitting up straighter to tell the story.

"Your mother was not my fire, remember? I'm sure she told you that, as well. I still thought we were happy together during the time we shared. We had our two beautiful baby girls and watched them grow into beautiful young women. I thought that Vladeric was the one for her." Desmond cleared his throat uncomfortably. "He was around her more than anyone and was her head guard following her around the castle. I heard horrible rumors from the other guards of what Vladeric did in private. I was going to send him away, but your mother stopped me. That's when I became jealous towards him. I was sure it was him! She was acting differently, happier with her life in the castle after we signed the Blood Treaty with Romule. She sent Vladeric away to Antiqua to be with him. But she took her own life that night. I scoured her room looking for answers and I found a single note made out to me. She explained that she knew she had been acting differently and I was wrong. Vladeric wasn't the one she had fallen for. The one she did fall for betrayed her for another woman and she couldn't take the pain of it. Your mother chose to end her own life that night, but to this day I still don't know who it was that caused that pain. I wish she would've talked to me. I can't tell you why she sent him here. The truth died along with her."

Odesha absorbed this. She had already known most of what he said, but asked softly, "Why did you send me here?"

Desmond smiled, sadly replying, "I knew the ice had chosen you and there was nothing to be done. I was so close to losing you, I couldn't think of anything else to do. I saw the spark enter your eyes when people spoke of Antiqua. You were interested. And I was right! You vanquished the man terrorizing your ancestral home, found the reason for the low profits, and fell in love! My little girl is back again." The tension from Desmond's face melted into a relieved smile. A small tear floated down Odesha's face. She *had* chosen the ice before she left for Antiqua, she could see that now. It had taken a lot to bring her away from it and she wasn't going back. Kunchok was her fire and he had ended her curse for good.

Odesha stood, holding out her hand to her father. He moved to his knees, placing his hand in her own to stand up. He held his arms open to her. Odesha hesitated for only a moment, rushing into his arms. It felt good to be held by him. It took her back to the days when she was little, and she would run to him if she had a scrape or wanted to tell on Vashti for any slight she made against her. She felt complete, having her father back. So, she was going to give him a small piece of himself back.

"Before Vladeric died he told me who mother had met," whispered Vashti. She hated bringing up old wounds, but sometimes a wound needed to be reopened to heal properly. Desmond stiffened, tightening his arms on his daughter.

"Who?" he gruffly asked. A part of him had always wanted to know the truth.

"The King of Romule. She met him while signing the Blood Treaty. I think the King advised mother to put Vladeric in Antiqua. The King told Vladeric to relay the message he would be with her there soon. But somehow she found out about the woman the King had married."

Desmond shuddered, silent in the light of the new information. His heart broke all over again, this new information bringing his loss to light again. She hadn't been his true love, but he had respected and loved both of his wives in their own individual way.

Odesha whispered, "No matter how much we want to change the past, we must look to the present to shape our future."

"When did my daughter become so wise?" Desmond asked, holding Odesha at arm's length to look her up and down with a smile. The information

Odesha had shared with him didn't change the past, she was right, but he did have closure. He had always felt like he had failed his first wife.

Odesha smiled brightly, "It must've been when I was flying over the mountain in the sharp grip of an orik. The world looked different from up there."

Desmond's booming laughter echoed throughout the hallway. "When do we celebrate your journey home?"

"How about you get some rest and we'll have the celebration tonight?" she promised. Desmond let out a whoop of excitement, kissing her on top of the head, and made his way to his room. He wanted to debut a new brew he had been working on.

Kunchok came further around the corner to leave his hiding place, eying Odesha happily. Her light blue gown made her eyes sparkle with color, clear of worry for the moment. It was rare to see. She cared so much for everyone around her and wished happiness for everyone that she neglected herself at times. That's why he watched her so closely. He wanted to look out for her when she didn't herself.

He cleared his throat.

Odesha turned, startled, and asked, "How long have you been there?" Raising an eyebrow, she waited for his reply.

"I heard everything." Smiling, he realized her

tongue was complicated, but he liked to understand everything she said now.

Odesha groaned. "You aren't supposed to listen to a private conversation, Kunchok," she grudgingly said.

"You are in the middle of the hallway; did you forget already?" He looked concerned, feeling her forehead with his hand. He looked especially handsome today wearing a deep-V tunic showing off his scars. It gave him a dashing appearance.

"No, I didn't forget. Let's go find Fanni. Maybe she knows where Mira is hiding. The celebration is tonight!" Odesha reminded him, tugging at his arm. He hadn't forgotten. The excitement was palpable in the castle. It was going to be a large celebration and it made him nervous to be a focal point in front of all the strangers. But this was for her.

Kunchok asked curiously, "You are not worried for Vashti?"

Odesha shook her head and replied, "No. Vashti looked like she had the situation semi-under control. She is tough. Stronger than any woman I know. She would cut you in two if you crossed her. I am worried for Saphira. I hope Endemion can find her quickly." She frowned, wondering where she could have gone.

"She isn't stronger than any woman I know,"

Kunchok said swiftly. "My wife is the strongest of women. She faced an orik, a storm, and magic beasts. She faced her fears and her family. I'm proud of you."

Odesha jumped up to wrap her arms around Kunchok's neck in her happiness. That was the nicest thing anyone had ever said to her. She was going to reward him later.

"When is the Prince leaving to find Saphira?" he asked with a smile. He didn't want her worrying herself to death over the situation, and he knew she would. If he could offer her his help before Endemion left, he would.

Odesha shrugged, "I was going to ask at the celebration. He needed time to prepare, so I'm sure he's not gone yet. I'm going to talk to him about us journeying with him."

"I thought you would. We'll go together," Kunchok replied decisively. He wasn't going to let her go unprotected, even though she had her powers. He would be just as worried as Endemion then, pacing the halls waiting for news. They left the castle together to find Dek and Fanni.

Odesha and Kunchok knocked on Dek and Fanni's new home. It was a small cottage with two rooms, perfect for the size of their family. If one day they decided to have more children, they could always build on or find a new home. The door opened wide, a happily smiling Fanni waiting at the doorway. Halana and Boni sat at the table talking animatedly with Dek and Dede.

Odesha yelled her greeting to the group. She hadn't seen them since arriving, being so busy, and she felt bad.

Halana stood, hugging Odesha tightly to her. She asked, "How was the Reawakening?"

"It went perfectly. The boy's illness went away, and he went home right after with his family. My sister called me to her at the end using the stone I gave her."

Halana's eyebrow shot up, giving Odesha a concerned look. She verified, "Is she well?"

Odesha sighed. "Yes and no. She seemed to be happy, but she was trying to make it through trials wherever she is. Vashti ordered Endemion to find our half-sister Saphira first. She is near the forests of Bijou and we need to search for her quickly. She is…gentle. Endemion is leading the rescue. Tonight, I'm going to ask if he needs assistance." She changed the subject, asking absently. "Have you seen Mira? I need to ask her about the preparations."

"Yes, I saw her at my brother Halafren's cottage visiting," Halana recalled.

Odesha stood abruptly, shocked. "At your

brother's home? The quiet man that hasn't said two words to me? That brother? Why didn't you tell me?"

Kunchok laughed and sipped his drink Dek had provided. He interrupted, "Halafren hardly ever speaks. He is a great provider, focused on the hunt. If you had approached him in the marketplace, he wouldn't have talked to you."

Halana nodded sheepishly. "Mira started asking him question after question about where he wanted to live and how he was liking Antiqua. I think he was shocked someone could talk so much. They have been…inseparable…ever since."

Fanni stood with a squeal and screamed, "Ranna soon?! She will need lessons, Halana!" What a wonderful idea to merge the two cultures. They could have two celebrations.

Odesha groaned, remembering her own "lessons." That had been chaos, but the memories were special to her. Father had said he was debuting a new brew tonight. Odesha worried Fanni would find a new loma she favored. She looked Fanni up and down, promising to have a word with Desmond about being a bad influence on the tribe.

"I'm going to go speak with Mira. Have a great day, everyone." Odesha stood, reaching over to grasp Kunchok's hand to lead him to the doorway. They waved to the group. It was nice to see Dek's shoulders free of worry and the happiness that shone brightly in Halana's and Fanni's eyes. Boni just seemed happy to have a family with Halana. He was accepted and loved.

Kunchok knocked on Halafren's cottage door. The smaller cottage was framed for a single man. Opening the door widely, a blushing Mira shyly greeted them. Halafren sat at the table carving an orik from a piece of wood. Odesha hadn't realized how much Halafren favored his sister before. His blue coloring matched hers, but the larger muscles and hairier face proclaimed him a male. The swirls of hair peppering his face were softer than Kunchok's making him seem more approachable. He looked up from his sculpture with his brown eyes, standing to greet them, worry clearly etched on his face.

"Good, chief?" he asked abruptly.

Kunchok nodded, smiling to ease his worry. He explained, "Odesha wanted to ask Mira about the preparations for the celebration tonight."

Mira gasped, turning to Odesha with her soft brown eyes, replying without question, "Yes, milady. Everything is ready. The cooks know what to prepare. Everyone is very excited to attend tonight. Gamble even gave the men the day off from mining!"

Halafren nodded, turning back to his craft, uninterested in the talk of celebrations. Odesha smiled at the soft look Mira gave Halafren. She didn't seem to mind that he didn't join their discussion.

Odesha softly suggested, "Come to the castle to get ready for the ceremony if you like, Mira. Halana and Fanni will be there with me."

Mira gasped at the honor the Princess bestowed upon her. She was getting ready with royalty!

"Thank you, Princess Odesha, of course I'll come."

CHAPTER 23

Kunchok went below to the celebration while the women got ready, wanting to find Endemion before Odesha did. He had to know what his plan was so he could stop worrying.

Endemion sat on the throne watching the people mill around him in their fine gowns. His mind was racing with all the preparations that needed to be done, secretly planning to leave as soon as possible without telling anyone but his own captain. He could move faster by himself than with a group of people. Getting out of the castle without being seen was going to be painful though. He rubbed his arm at what was coming.

Odesha's new husband walked towards him. The tunic fit him well, his large furred muscles stretching out the outfit nicely. He was kind, this ice fey from the north. Endemion was happy to have him in the family, even if he didn't show it to his sister. It was a sound match filled with promise. He expected a niece or nephew to be produced from the union soon, but first he would guarantee their safety by wiping out all who stood to harm them all.

Kunchok growled softly, "You plan to leave soon."

Endemion crossed his legs, settling down for a long talk and asked, "Is that a question or a fact?"

"A fact. It is what I would do. You want to move fast across your vast land but can't use a large force to show your presence. Odesha wants to join you, by the way. And if she goes, I go," Kunchok stated emphatically, settling in for the discussion by sitting on the queen's throne beside Endemion.

Endemion rolled his eyes, snarling softly, "Why does everyone want to get in my way?!"

"Because she cares about you." Desmond sidled up beside the group talking, burping unexpectedly. "I think your sister is ready for the journey. She's proved she's just as strong as you, Endemion. Give her a chance to prove herself! You have to rely on the people around you, haven't I told you this before?"

"Spare me your 'suggestions' father. It is hard to

rely on the people around you when they aren't reliable," Endemion bit out.

Kunchok eyed his new brother. He carried a lot of baggage for someone so young and it was wearing on him. Endemion reminded him of Dek, needing someone to shoulder the burden with him. The King wasn't helping his son, only interested in revelry. The times that Desmond showed his wisdom were few and far between.

Kunchok interjected before the argument became heated. "I have been wanting to see your land. Odesha and I could go to find Saphira and you find Vashti. Odesha knows this world better than I. We will take a small guard and travel quickly."

Desmond took a swig of his large drink, smacking his lips at the tasty liquid. He asked, "Why wouldn't you go to Vashti instead, Endemion?"

Endemion rubbed his head. It was beginning to pain him to voice his thoughts to the group. He was used to talking to himself in silence.

He replied, "Because Odesha can't stand the heat of Baklan. It would be like a heat dungeon to her."

"She faced Vladeric in a heat dungeon. When will you give your sister credit? It's like the squabbles you four used to engage in when you were younger!" Desmond argued.

Endemion snarled, "I won't let Odesha come to

harm! She will find Saphira and I will go to Baklan. It's too dangerous there! I can meet Odesha at the Bijou Forest and travel with her from there."

"NO. We will go to Baklan." The shout was loud enough to fill the entire throne room.

A woman walked towards them. Wearing only tight black clothing, with a symbol of a flame on her breast, she walked confidently to the throne while passing the gaping crowd. Her short pixie hair stood out among the people, her graceful steps carrying her before the Prince. The Prince leaned forward, interested at what the tiny sprite had to say.

"Why would I go to Baklan with a pixie?" asked Endemion curiously.

The lady snorted, but still replied, "The better question is, why would I let you come with me?" She continued to walk to the throne.

Endemion laughed menacingly. "Nobody lets me do anything, they are told what to do. I have the power here. Who do I have the…pleasure…of meeting?" He lifted a brow, waiting on what retort she would use next. Sparring with the sprite was invigorating.

She lifted her nose in the air and hesitated. "Rainey of the Incendie Tanssijja." A gasp echoed through the throne room. An Incendie was a fire dancer from Romule, an assassin trained in the arts.

"Ah. That explains much then," Endemion acknowledged sarcastically.

Kunchok tilted his head. He asked, "Why would you want to go to Baklan?" The female eyed the fey up and down, raising a surprised brow at his position in the queen's throne beside the Prince.

"I'll make a bargain with you, Prince. I will tell you everything I know if you help me find Vashti and Saphira," Rainey announced, ignoring Kunchok.

Endemion leaned forward, his forearms placed on his knees. He watched her thoughtfully. A slow smile edged his mouth, his sharp teeth apparent. It reminded Kunchok of a cow beast about to attack.

"And why would I make a bargain with Princess Rainey of Romule?" Several of the miners present paled at Endemion's revelation. They remembered the Blood War well. Their family members had been taken to Romule only to pass under horrifying circumstances. They had paid the price of Romule's blood magic and wanted no part of any of their ilk. The Blood Treaty was a shaky one at best, forged under pressure from both sides many years ago. The whispers of the miners increased throughout the room, the people wondering why Rainey would be here. What was she hiding? The people were terrified of what her presence meant.

Kunchok worried about his brother being alone

with her if what he had heard about the Blood War was true. He moved to tell the Prince of his concern, when Endemion held his hand up to stop him, tilting his head in thought. Kunchok winced, knowing whatever the Prince had decided wouldn't be good for Rainey, no matter what she thought. Her bargain had been in the Prince's favor.

"You have a bargain, Princess," Endemion answered finally.

She shook her head, her short hair feathering across her face. She placed her hands on her hips. Rainey stood up straight with her slight form and informed him, "Just Rainey, please, Your Highness. I am here only as an Incendie."

"Very well. You will be treated as an Incendie would, then." Endemion stood up to shake her hand. He held out his clawed hand, waiting to see what she would do. His long sleeves and cloak hid most of his form from view. "Be ready to leave tonight after the celebration. I seem to find myself in a rush." She took his hand firmly, his rough hand giving her pause. Having thought to meet a pampered scholar, finding instead a warrior swirling with black magic, had changed everything. It unnerved her.

"I'll be ready, Prince Endemion," she replied, a shiver racing through her voice that she tried to hide. But he knew. His sinister smile told her as much.

He leaned forward, still holding her hand, whispering for her ears only, "And so will I."

Rainey blushed, wondering at his meaning. He released her hand. "Have some food and drink, Incendie. The main attraction is about to start." Rainey nodded, turning away from the throne room, threading through the people that continued to stare at her as if she had three heads. It made her uncomfortable, just like everywhere else she went. She kept her head high, going to the drink table to sip the brew lightly. She coughed when it hit her tongue, the strong flavor bursting through her mouth.

"Good, eh? My own recipe." The dark demon beside her enjoying himself pointed towards her drink.

She swallowed roughly, but her answer was truthful, "It's something I've never experienced before." It was vile.

"Ah ha! I told them all it would be the latest rage in Antiqua." He held out his hand to shake hers. "I'm Desmond."

Rainey sputtered, dropping into a curtsy hurriedly. "Your…Your Majesty! It is an honor to meet you!"

He shushed her, looking around, ordering, "Just Desmond in private. If you can just be an Incendie, I can just be Desmond, right?" His wild uncombed hair looked strange with his appearance. He looked like he had gotten dressed backwards, without a mirror to help guide him. The clothing didn't exactly match, but he had the softest eyes. Like a newborn puppy.

"R…right," Rainey agreed. A trumpet sounded its call, announcing the arrival of Princess Odesha and her entourage. Rainey took a deep gulp of the brew she held to the encouragement of Desmond.

It was going to be a long night.

CHAPTER 24

Fanni threw Odesha's door open without knocking, the new loma she had been introduced to by Desmond swirling precariously over the side of the giant chalice she had acquired. It had been a welcome present to Antiqua.

Also, from Desmond.

He had become a favorite of hers. They shared the same interests, mainly loma. Dek always accompanied them on their jaunts, keeping both of his unruly charges safe, even from themselves. They made a great trio. Fanni was already planning on introducing them to some of her tribe members. She believed Desmond was just lonely, that's why he was so jovial all the time. He was hiding a broken heart, but she hadn't voiced her options to Dek yet. In her heart, she knew she was right.

"I brought some loma for you to try, Halana. Oh! What's wrong with Mira?!" Fanni hurried inside. She placed her chalice on the bedside table to keep it safe. Mira was bent over at the waist, sobbing on Odesha's old bed. Kunchok and Odesha had recently moved into the larger master bedroom, but this was the room the group had chosen to get ready in.

Halana tried to talk over the sounds Mira was making. She patted Mira on the back softly. "Mira… was asked questions by Halafren about Ranna. Mira is upset because there is no way she could be with Halafren unless she learned Ranna." Fanni froze, startling Odesha. She let out a whoop of excitement. Fanni ran to the other side of Mira, landing on the bed with a bounce.

Fanni yelled out, "I knew it! We had discussed this earlier, Mira. You have nothing to worry about. We helped Odesha with her dance and we will help you with yours." Odesha handed her a handkerchief to mop her tears.

Mira blew her nose and whispered brokenly, "You…you will?"

"Of course, we will help," Halana said. "I love my brother very much. If he wants to be with you, and you him, I will help." Mira stopped her crying, crisis averted, hugging both Fanni and Halana to herself. She blushed, apologizing to Odesha for her behavior.

Odesha reassured her, "Don't be sorry, Mira! I'm glad you're happy with Halafren. We'll work on your dance after the celebration."

Mira nodded her head. She said, "Your Highness, I brought fabric up from the royal coffers for Halana to craft. I hope you don't mind. I had heard she is quite skilled, so I wanted to use her services."

Odesha waved her hand, dismissing Mira's concerns about the cloth. She should have thought of that herself. "It's alright, Mira. We have enough fabric down there to clothe the entire tribe if necessary. We need to use it before it mildews."

Halana excitedly stood, reaching for the packages she had with her. She was nervous to show her friends what she had made for them. For Fanni she had made a long, yellow dress. It was a conservative piece that fell off her shoulders becomingly. Halana had made herself a knee-length, rose-colored dress that fell in soft pleats. Mira's was a harder one to craft. It was ice blue, falling in soft waves to her feet. Odesha's dress was special. It was purely white with sparkling beading threaded throughout the skirt. The fitted top was littered with the sparkles.

Each dress matched their wearer perfectly. They

each dressed behind the screen individually, chatting away while the celebration became louder. When they were done, they each filed out separately down the stairs.

Odesha waited until her friends left, fixing pieces of her straight hair that had separated. She fastened the empty bloodstone around her neck, thinking of Vashti.

As Odesha walked down the stairs, the music died down to a soft lull. The crowd became quiet, a hush descending through them. Desmond waited at the bottom of the stairs for Odesha. She looked curiously at him. When his hand reached out to take her own, she became worried.

"What's going on?" Odesha whispered. The smiles and stares from the crowd of miners and fey were unnerving. Gamble was mopping at the tears in his eyes. Mira patted him on the back. Odesha didn't understand why everyone was so emotional.

"Now don't be upset, dear heart," Desmond reasoned, leading her to the end of the room. The crowd parted, allowing their regents by them.

"You're scaring me." Odesha tried to peer around people to find Kunchok. Maybe Endemion was testing his magic out on him again. She stopped walking; the scene in front of her caused her to fall against her father in awe. The entire room was decorated in beautiful swaths of white fabric. Beautiful flowers of pale rose with ivy flowing from the stems littered the tables and walls. In the center of their destination stood Kunchok. Beside him, Endemion stood. A rare smile graced his face.

Desmond leaned down to whisper, "Are you ready to get married? Kunchok planned this with Endemion. He wanted to give you the wedding you deserved, in our custom. He wanted to be joined to you every way he could."

"What about Vashti and Saphira?" Odesha worried out loud. She wanted them to be by her side. It didn't feel complete without them.

Desmond straightened. He knew she would miss her sisters. "I wish they were both here. We had planned for them to be a part of the celebration. I suggested to Kunchok to have two ceremonies where we would all be present. This could be a joining of houses, of worlds together finding each other again."

Odesha nodded, relieved. She grasped Desmond's outstretched elbow. Dede and Evie walked towards them, holding a beautiful bouquet of flowers for Odesha to carry. They held their smaller bouquets, moving in front of the adults to guide them towards the walkway lined with flowers. Odesha's hand shook with her nerves. It had been a secret dream of hers to have a beautiful wedding to the man of her dreams, and it was finally happening.

She was marrying her husband all over again. Desmond and Odesha walked down the makeshift aisle of people standing at attention. Halana, Fanni, and Mira stood beside Endemion. They held candles, a symbol of the couple's undying love. At the side of Kunchok stood Dek, Boni, and Halafren with folded hands held on their swords, a symbol of their trust.

Odesha reached the end of the aisle, looking for a place to put her flowers. A lone girl with short hair stood by herself uncomfortably. Odesha reached out to her, placing the flowers gently in her arms.

Rainey stared down at the flowers in horror. She had never met the Princess before, and the flowers landing in her arms seemed like an omen. When she looked up at Endemion to judge his reaction, his eyes that had been watching her shifted away.

Kunchok walked towards Odesha, nodding to

Desmond respectfully. He grabbed her hands to lead her towards Endemion. He watched her face the entire time. Endemion softly began the marriage rites that had been taught to him through his training. Staring into her eyes, Kunchok marveled at how far they had come since he had first seen her running through the forest, a blood trail leading him to the cave she hid in. He had a family. The tribe had a home. They had plentiful food and tasks the people loved to do. He was in love with his beautifully brave mate and would cherish her for eternity, he promised in his pledge. Odesha watched her husband make his promise, her own love shining brightly in her eyes. She was sad her sisters weren't there, but inside her heart they would always stay. They were there in spirit. Vowing her own love, her thankfulness that she had found him, and her own promise to be at his side through any trial, she showed her people that their differences didn't matter. They were one in each other's hearts.

After the vows were exchanged, the musicians struck up a soft melody. Their instruments strummed a beautiful sound. Kunchok softly kissed her mouth, guiding her to the center dance floor in front of the throne. He took her hand, holding her waist as they danced across the floor to their own rhythm, smiling softly to each other. More couples twirled on the floor joining them in their celebration.

"Are you happy?" Kunchok whispered, leaning into her embrace.

Odesha smiled. "This was a dream of mine, to have a happy life with my husband who loves me. The reality is better than the dream. I can't imagine my life without you. I still can't believe you put this all together." She looked around in wonder at all the details he had added through the room.

"I did this for us. I wanted the whole tribe to see our love." He leaned down to brush his lips against her own. Her heart swelled with the emotion that crowded inside her.

He cleared his throat and whispered, "Would you mind if we retired early tonight?"

"Not at all," answered Odesha quickly. A tingle of anticipation raced through her.

Kunchok nodded. "Good, because we are leaving tonight. We are going to go on a journey."

"We are?" Odesha asked, confused.

"We need to rescue my new sister," Kunchok said with a smile. Odesha laughed joyously, jumping into his arms to the cheer of the crowd.

"I love you, Kunchok. Now and forever. Let's go on our adventure."

"I love you more, Odesha. Vo lo cos suti ba suta."

The couple made their way up the stairs to exit their wedding with a flourish, sealing their love with soft kisses and promises they planned to keep…forever.

THE END

COMING SOON…
VASHTI'S STORY

AUTHOR'S NOTE

I hope you enjoyed Odesha and Kunchok's story! Vashti's story is next. After that, we will visit Saphira. Endemion, that complicated soul, will be last. You will get to read about Odesha and Kunchok, together again, in Saphira's story. The Reawakening scene, when Vashti calls Odesha, will be in the second book. (Why did Vashti need her?) We can't forget Esmerelda! She left a lot of clues to what is going to happen next. I love that spunky pirate! Maybe someone else will love her too…

GLOSSARY

Kaia (place)- The entire world

Merdi (place)- A multi-cultural kingdom between Antiqua and Romule, includes a shipping port, ruler is King Desmond

Romule- Kingdom of the magisters, began the blood war, ruler is King Rion

Antiqua- The northernmost kingdom, multi-cultural, the people mainly mine salt for Merdi

Baklan- The southernmost kingdom of Kaia. Neighbors Romule.

Forest of Bijou- Borders Romule and Baklan.

Blood Treaty- A peaceful agreement signed between Romule and Merdi to end the Blood War

Reawakening- Ritual to convert vampire

children from food to blood. It is needed when the child becomes sick.

Orik- Large stork-like bird that builds nests in bundles that hang on snow trees branches. It has metal plates and grey/white feathers.

Evian- Bird used to deliver messages. They were used by families across kingdoms during the Blood War.

Bloodstone- A clear crystal that can accept blood from a donor. The donor can be summoned by whoever has the stone, until the blood dries.

Incendie Tanssijja- A fire dancer from Romule. Some call them assassins.

LANGUAGE GLOSSARY

Bulvo- Hunter
Shousha- Soul
Densho- Silence
Lisha vo- Thank you
Dunka ari ro bov- Stay with or die
Yemi- Eat
Vo riwa- You sleep
Vo lo cos suti ba suta- You are mine now and forever.
Loma- A drink similar to alcohol
Ramdak- Banishment

ABOUT THE AUTHOR

Alia Johnson was born in Southern Illinois to two amazing parents that took her on different adventures every year. She used to love cheerleading under the lights of the home football games when her husband played. (Check out his fishing page Carp'n.) They have two amazingly talented children who surprise her every day. She is best friends with her brother, hates when her food touches, loves gardening, and plans to keep showing her readers the experiences that visit her every night while she dreams. Thank you, Mr. Sandman. You will always be my muse.

Facebook Page | Email | Official Website

Made in the USA
Monee, IL
14 September 2020